TAKING SIDES

"Who do you think Jeffrey likes better," Jenny asked curiously, "Enid or Lila?"

"*Enid?*" Jessica demanded, horrified. "Why would he like *Enid?*"

Jessica's cousin's brown eyes widened. "Well, I thought Elizabeth was trying to help Enid get together with him. I heard—" She broke off when she saw the expression on Jessica's face. "Did I say something wrong?"

"No, Jen," Jessica said grimly. "What did you hear?"

Jenny looked uncomfortable. "Well, I accidentally overheard Elizabeth talking to Enid on the phone. And she kept encouraging Enid, saying that she was a million times better suited to Jeffrey than Lila."

"Oh, she did, did she?" Jessica seethed. So *that* was Elizabeth's plan! Well, she wasn't going to let Elizabeth outmaneuver her. Not in a million years!

Bantam Books in the Sweet Valley High Series
Ask your bookseller for the books you have missed

SWEET VALLEY HIGH

TAKING SIDES

Written by
Kate William

Created by
FRANCINE PASCAL

BANTAM BOOKS
TORONTO · NEW YORK · LONDON · SYDNEY · AUCKLAND

RL 6, IL age 12 and up

TAKING SIDES

A Bantam Book / October 1986

Sweet Valley High is a trademark of Francine Pascal

Conceived by Francine Pascal

Produced by Cloverdale Press Inc.
133 Fifth Ave. New York, N.Y. 10003

Cover art by James Mathewuse

ISBN 0-553-25886-9

Published simultaneously in the United States and Canada

PRINTED IN THE UNITED STATES OF AMERICA

O   11 10 9 8 7 6 5 4 3 2 1

To Monika Block,
with love from her
sister Rachel

One

"Elizabeth, you're blocking the sun!" Jessica Wakefield complained, shading her aquamarine eyes and squinting critically at her twin sister.

Elizabeth laughed. "Twins are supposed to share things, right?" she reminded her. "At least that's what you told me this morning, when you borrowed that bracelet you're wearing. You'd think we'd be able to share the sunlight, too!"

Lila Fowler giggled. "She's got you there, Jess," she pointed out. "Anyway, you shouldn't get too comfortable. Lunch hour's almost over, and you promised you'd help me with my history homework before next period."

Jessica groaned. "Can't a girl even relax for a minute around this place?" she complained, pulling herself up to a sitting position. The girls were on the grassy front lawn in front of Sweet Valley High, listening to Lila's cassette player and enjoying the sunshine before afternoon classes began.

"Speaking of sharing," Jessica said suddenly. "Robin was saying the cheerleaders really need to try our new routine to music. Could I borrow your cassette player this afternoon, Lila? I promise I'll give it back to you tomorrow," she added.

Lila shrugged. "Take it all week," she said nonchalantly. "Daddy's got about five of them at home. He'll never even notice this one's gone."

"See, Liz!" Jessica said triumphantly. "*That's* what I call generosity."

Elizabeth exchanged an amused smile with Enid Rollins, her best friend, who was sitting with them on the lawn. She could think of a few more appropriate labels for Lila's behavior! It was easy enough to be generous when one's allowance was the size Lila's was. The only daughter of one of the richest men in Southern California, Lila Fowler had only to point to something, and it was hers. Sometimes Elizabeth felt sorry for Lila, though. She knew the girl must be

2

lonely. Her parents were divorced, and she hadn't seen her mother in years. Her father traveled a lot, so often her only companion in the huge mansion in which they lived was the housekeeper.

Elizabeth tended to give people the benefit of the doubt; thus, she had always tried to make allowances for Lila's behavior. But it was hard to sympathize when Lila carried on as she usually did, bragging about her clothes or her new personal computer, going on and on about the lavish vacations she and her father went on, or making snide comments about her classmates.

Elizabeth sighed, her gaze moving past Lila to her sister Jessica. Looking at Jessica was like looking into a mirror. Juniors at Sweet Valley High, the sixteen-year-old twins were identical: slender and willowy, with sun-streaked blond hair tumbling down to their shoulders and wideset blue-green eyes. They had the kind of looks that make California girls famous around the world.

One helpful distinguishing feature was that Elizabeth dressed much more conservatively than her sister. Elizabeth usually preferred tailored skirts and sweaters, chinos, or jeans, the kind of comfortable classic clothing that Jessica declared unfit to wear anywhere outside the house—although Jessica felt free to borrow anything that appealed to her, since she went through style after style with relentless enthusiasm.

And that, Elizabeth reflected, was probably characteristic of the main difference between them. She considered herself dedicated, hardworking, and liked taking things one step at a time. She loved her schoolwork and took her hobbies seriously, especially her work for *The Oracle*, the school newspaper. Elizabeth hoped to be a writer one day, and she knew she needed all the experience she could get. She kept a journal, too, where she recorded her innermost thoughts and the events that mattered most to her. Elizabeth had dozens of friends, but she valued her privacy as well. She enjoyed being on her own or with her best friend, Enid Rollins, who shared many of her interests, rather than with a large group.

Jessica, on the other hand, thought Enid Rollins was too boring for words. Jessica loved crowds and excitement, and it wasn't surprising that *her* hobbies usually put her in the limelight. Co-captain of the cheerleaders with Robin Wilson, Jessica did everything she could to maintain what she called her "visibility." Whatever Jessica's latest obsession was—modern dance, gourmet cooking, matchmaking, or just the inevitable shopping spree—she was sure to throw herself into it with great if short-lived enthusiasm.

Elizabeth loved her sister with all her might, despite their occasional squabbles and their constant differences of opinion. And what she admired most about Jessica was her enthusiasm, which could flare up at any minute and change a dull day into an adventure-filled one.

"Hey," Jessica said suddenly, her eyes sparkling as if she had been reading her sister's mind. "Isn't that the new guy from Oregon over there with Aaron Dallas?"

Elizabeth followed her sister's gaze. "You're right," she said matter-of-factly, then turned and smiled at Enid. Enid blushed and looked away, obviously trying to look nonchalant.

"He was at the party you guys had for Steve, right?" Lila said, putting on her sunglasses and staring across the lawn. The party Lila was referring to had taken place a week earlier and had been given by the twins for their older brother Steven to mark the end of his midterm break from college, where he was in his freshman year. Steven had been seriously considering leaving school to take a job on the cruise ship owned by his roommate's father, and the

Wakefields had all been involved in a scheme to change his mind. Luckily their plan had worked, and Steven had decided to carry on with his education and put plans of work off for the present.

"Jeffrey French," Jessica said dreamily. "What a wonderful name. He's got to be really romantic with a name like *French*."

Elizabeth laughed. "Well, he sure is good-looking," she said, hoping to close the discussion. She knew how uncomfortable it must be making Enid feel. Jeffrey had been at school for only a week, but he had already made a big impression. He had come to the Friday the Thirteenth dance put on by the school committee a week before, and Enid had noticed him right away. The next night he had come to the party at the Wakefields' house with Aaron Dallas, a classmate of the twins. Aaron and Jeffrey had been at the same soccer camp the summer before. Elizabeth had only to take one look at Enid that night to know she'd been hit—and hit hard. It had been a long time since Enid had cared for someone, and Elizabeth had often suspected that when it happened, it would happen with a vengeance. And she had been right: Enid had already confided to Elizabeth that she liked Jeffrey. In fact, Elizabeth and Enid had been scheming for days, trying to think of a good way for Enid and Jeffrey to get a real chance to talk.

"He sure *is* cute," Lila said, studying Jeffrey and letting her history book slip unnoticed off her lap. "Where's he from? Why haven't I gotten to meet him yet?"

Elizabeth frowned. "He's from Oregon," she said, thinking fast. The last thing Enid needed was for Lila to get interested in Jeffrey!

"He's from a farm," Enid chimed in, winking at Elizabeth.

Elizabeth giggled, taking the hint. Lila would never be interested in Jeffrey if they played up his outdoorsy nature. Lila liked slick, sophisticated guys—usually older than she was—with hefty bank accounts. "That's right," Elizabeth confirmed. "He's a soccer player. That's how he knows Aaron. He's really crazy about sports—anything outdoors and athletic."

"He sounds divine," Lila said. "No wonder he's got such huge muscles." She hugged herself and smiled. "I bet he's got a really sensitive side to him. Isn't that what you always hear about farm boys?"

Elizabeth and Enid looked at each other, dismayed. "I don't think so, Lila," Enid said hurriedly. "I think farming is pretty gross, actually.

Lots of manure and smelly animals and everything."

Lila didn't look the least bit perturbed. "Oh, animals," she said flippantly. "Daddy says the out-of-doors is the best place for a young man to build character."

Jessica couldn't suppress a groan. She knew that Lila's father hated nature. But Lila ignored her. She slipped her sunglasses off and studied herself critically in her compact mirror. "I wonder if he likes horses. Daddy mentioned that he'd like to get me a horse, but I haven't ridden one in so long. Maybe Jeffrey can help me out."

Jessica looked delighted. "Lila, what a great idea! And who knows, maybe one thing will lead to another. You and Jeffrey French would make the best couple ever!"

Elizabeth bit her lip. "Oh, I don't think so," she said, trying not to show how upset she was. Enid looked horrified.

"Why not?" Lila demanded. "I need to meet a *real* guy, you know what I mean? I'm sick of pretentious college men. I want someone earnest, someone sincere—"

"Lila," Elizabeth cut in, "do you really think you'd like a guy whose favorite pastimes are mountain climbing and soccer?"

"Absolutely," Lila said stubbornly. "Daddy and I climbed mountains once when we were skiing in the Alps. It was a really wonderful experience, Liz." She looked hurt. "You guys don't give me enough credit. I'm sick of boys with big trust funds who don't care about the real things in life. Jeffrey French is exactly the sort of guy I need!"

"Bravo!" Jessica shrieked, clapping her hands. "Lila, let's go over and I'll introduce you. You're going to just adore him, I can tell!"

"I can tell, too," Lila said enthusiastically, gathering her books together and scrambling to her feet. The next minute she and Jessica were hurrying across the lawn, talking animatedly as they closed in on Jeffrey French.

Elizabeth sighed as she watched them approach the handsome blond boy. "Enid," she said, patting her friend's hand sympathetically, "you must be ready to kill her!"

Enid's green eyes flashed. "I can't believe my rotten luck, Liz. Lila could go after any guy she wanted. Why does she have to go for the one guy in the whole world I'm interested in?"

Elizabeth looked thoughtfully at Enid. "Well, there's no point in giving up," she said cheerfully.

"What do you mean?" Enid said glumly.

"Lila's got everything: cars, credit cards, an incredible mansion! How in the world am I supposed to compete with all *that*?"

Elizabeth giggled. "Lila doesn't have Elizabeth Wakefield on her side," she pointed out. "And I'll tell you something, Enid. *I* am not going to sit back and watch that girl walk all over poor Jeffrey!"

Enid began to look a bit more like her old self. "Do you really think I've got a chance?" she asked dubiously.

"I don't just think so," Elizabeth said confidently. "I *know* so!"

"Jessica, hurry up!" Elizabeth called, watching her twin stroll leisurely across the sun-dappled parking lot. Elizabeth was in the passenger seat of the red Fiat Spider she and her sister shared.

"Boy, you're a real grouch today," Jessica commented, throwing her cheerleading sweater and Lila's cassette recorder in the back of the car and climbing in. "What's the big hurry?" she asked as she turned the key in the ignition.

"I guess you've forgotten all about Jenny," Elizabeth said accusingly.

Jessica's aqua eyes widened, and she clapped

her hand over her mouth. "Oh, no," she groaned. "You're right. I did forget! No wonder you're so crabby!"

Elizabeth laughed. "Jenny's a perfectly nice girl," she declared. "And I'm *not* in a bad mood at all. I just promised Mom we'd be home in time to help with dinner tonight. Dad's picking Jenny up at the airport and bringing her back with him on his way home from work."

"Poor Dad." Jessica unwrapped a stick of gum and popped it into her mouth, then started the car. "Can you imagine anything worse after a long week at the office than having to suffer through a car ride alone with Jenny Townsend?"

Elizabeth shook her head as her twin backed the Fiat out of the parking lot. "She's your cousin, Jess," she said reprovingly. "It isn't really nice to talk about her that way. Besides, we haven't seen her in ages. Maybe she's gotten better."

"Well," Jessica said moodily, "she couldn't have gotten any worse, that's for sure. Liz, don't you remember what she was like when she came last time? She wrecked that gorgeous blue skirt of mine, and she completely trashed my room—"

Elizabeth burst out laughing. Jessica's room

11

was infamous in the Wakefield household. The rest of the split-level ranch house was immaculate, but Jessica's room was always a mess. Elizabeth couldn't imagine that even Jenny could make it look worse than usual.

"I don't think it's funny," Jessica said with a pout. "She's completely impossible, Liz. And the worst part of the whole thing is that she never lets me out of her sight! She follows me around like—like—"

"Like she's your younger cousin and she looks up to you," Elizabeth said firmly. "Remember what Mom said, Jess. You'd better be nice to her."

"But she's staying for two whole weeks!" Jessica moaned. "I can't believe it! You'd think the girl would be a little more sensitive and at least shorten the misery for us."

"Jessica," Elizabeth warned.

"Why can't she look up to *you*? Or to Steve, for that matter? It's just my luck to have the nerdiest cousin in the whole world!"

"Well, we're just going to have to put up with her," Elizabeth said absently. Her mind was only partly occupied with Jessica's complaints. Elizabeth had been hard at work on a special supplement *The Oracle* was preparing for Food-Drive Week, a program set up in conjunction with the PTA to help raise money and food for needy families in the area. For the next two weeks, it looked as if *The Oracle* would demand even more of Elizabeth's time than it usually did. She was also thinking about Enid and wondering what, if anything, she could do to bring her friend and Jeffrey French together.

"It's the worst possible timing, too," Jessica continued as she drove. "There's the volleyball game against Parker High next week and the beach party for Food-Drive Week—and on top of all that, what am I going to do about *Eddie*?"

Elizabeth studied her twin for a minute. "Eddie?" she asked at last. "I hate to seem stupid, but who's Eddie?"

"Eddie Winters," Jessica said, "just happens to be the most totally important thing to have happened to me all year. If you weren't so wrapped up in that silly newspaper you'd probably know about him."

Elizabeth giggled. She couldn't help being amused by the tone of her sister's voice. Jessica fell in love almost as often as she changed her clothing! "Well, we all have to make sacrifices." Seeing the sad expression on her twin's face, Elizabeth added, "Don't look so glum, Jess. Is Eddie that tall guy I saw you with in the hall this afternoon?"

Jessica nodded. "He's a senior—and on the swim team. He's amazing, Liz. I'm not kidding. I think he's really the man of my dreams. I was practically sure he was going to ask me out sometime this weekend. Only now Jenny's coming, and everything's ruined!"

"Give the girl a chance," Elizabeth suggested. "She's fifteen now. She's not a baby anymore."

Jessica snorted. "That girl is a pain, Liz. A real pain. She's not going to be any better just 'cause she's two years older."

"Well, you'll certainly get a chance to find out," Elizabeth said. "Mom tried to convince Jenny to stay in my room, but apparently she refused. She said one of the things she liked best about coming out here to visit was sleeping in *your* room. So you two will get to see an awful lot of each other!"

Jessica turned the car into the Wakefield driveway and shut off the motor. Still holding on to the steering wheel, she closed her eyes and shook her head slowly, an expression of utter agony on her face. "Why me?" she wailed melodramatically. "Why is this happening to me?"

But Elizabeth was already out of the car and didn't bother to respond to her sister's theatrics. She was trying to think what she was going to say when Enid called her before dinner. She was still trying to come up with a good way to get Enid and Jeffrey together, before Lila got to the new boy first.

Two

"I don't know, Liz," Enid said disconsolately. "I don't think I've got much of a chance. Jeffrey's one in a million. How in the world am I going to get someone like him interested in me?"

Elizabeth was on the phone in her bedroom, her shoes kicked off and her legs tucked up under her. "Enid Rollins, I can't believe you! I've never heard you say anything so ridiculous. Can you imagine any guy in his right mind preferring Lila Fowler to you? You're sweet, sincere, clever, witty—everything a nice guy like Jeffrey would naturally care about! And, Lila! Well, you know Lila," she concluded.

"You've got a point there," Enid admitted.

"Lila isn't the world's easiest person to get along with. But you've got to admit the package sure looks good."

Elizabeth sighed. "Well, you know Lila's theory on life: 'Anything worth doing is worth overdoing.' I wouldn't put it past her to do anything to get Jeffrey if she's really interested in him. But that just means we have to be prepared with a counterattack."

Enid was quiet for a minute. "I don't know, Liz. I'm not sure I'm up for that sort of thing. Maybe Jeffrey and I just weren't meant for each other."

Elizabeth wrapped the telephone cord around her index finger. "You're just getting scared," she accused her friend. "Come on, Enid. Don't wimp out on me now!"

Enid sighed. "Well, it *has* been a long time," she reminded her friend. "I guess maybe I'm feeling a little nervous. I haven't had the best luck with guys, you know."

Elizabeth bit her lip, remembering what Enid had been through with her boyfriend George. That was all history now, but it had been incredibly painful at the time. George Warren and Enid had been together for a long time. When George fell for Robin Wilson, a classmate of theirs at Sweet Valley High, he had tried to spare Enid's

18

feelings by denying his change of heart. But everything came out after a terrible plane accident. George had just gotten his pilot's license and had rented a plane to take Enid for a ride. When it crashed, Enid was temporarily paralyzed. Eventually she regained the full use of her legs after she realized, with Elizabeth's help, that she was suffering from a psychological block. Subconsciously she had felt that as long as she was paralyzed, George would stay around.

It had been an especially painful lesson to learn, and Enid had been reluctant to get involved with anyone since George. She had had her share of dates, but they had all been casual. As she had confided in Elizabeth more than once, her independence had come only with a struggle. She wasn't certain she was ready to fall in love again.

Actually, Elizabeth and Enid shared some similar feelings in that department, and they often confided their fears to each other. Elizabeth also knew how it felt to lose someone who mattered a great deal. Like Enid, she had been involved with one special boy for a long time. When Todd Wilkins moved to Vermont, Elizabeth was devastated. Their initial decision to maintain their relationship despite the distance proved disastrous, but Elizabeth hadn't met anyone since

Todd. It was so hard to imagine really caring about a guy again; going through all the nervous, jittery feelings at the start, all the potential heartache. . . .

"Don't worry," she said to Enid. "I know it's scary, but it's definitely worthwhile."

"If you say so," Enid said uncertainly.

"I got a pretty good hint this afternoon that I wanted to tell you about," Elizabeth confided, dropping her voice a little. "Apparently Jeffrey's a terrific photographer, and Mr. Collins wants to recruit him to help us out on *The Oracle*. We could use a second photographer."

Enid's voice brightened. "That means you'll have a chance to get to know him better! Oh, Liz, that's wonderful!"

"Now," Elizabeth said, "we just have to make sure that *you* get to know him better. The minute that happens, I guarantee you that sparks are going to fly!"

Enid giggled. "You are the world's greatest friend, Elizabeth Wakefield."

Elizabeth smiled. More than anything, she wanted to make Enid happy. And whatever it took, she was going to do her best to get Enid and Jeffrey French together!

* * *

"We're home!" Mr. Wakefield called, slipping out of his jacket as he came into the front hallway.

Jessica rolled her eyes at Elizabeth. "Goodbye, peace and quiet," she said dramatically.

Elizabeth suppressed a giggle. "Come on," she protested. "Give the poor kid a chance."

But her words were lost in the shrill cry that Jenny emitted as she dashed into the living room to engulf her cousins in a huge hug. "Jess! Liz! I haven't seen either of you in *ages!*" she hollered, covering Jessica with kisses.

Jessica disentangled herself and sat down on the couch, trying to keep her expression neutral as she examined her cousin from head to foot. The years hadn't really changed Jenny, unfortunately, Jessica thought. Thick glasses, unkempt hair, at *least* ten pounds overweight, and dressed in the most unflattering fuchsia sweats, Jenny was, as far as Jessica was concerned, a mess. An absolute *mess*. Jessica would have loved to have a glamorous cousin like Lila's cousin Christopher. The only thing glamorous about Jenny was that she lived in Dallas. But that, Jessica reflected, didn't seem to have rubbed off on the unfortunate creature. Watching her careen joyfully around the living room, Jessica felt her heart

21

sink. The next two weeks were going to be even worse than she had feared.

"You look gorgeous, Jess," Jenny said admiringly, heaving herself down on the couch and stroking Jessica's angora sweater. Jessica frowned and inched away from her. The very worst thing about Jenny was that she just *adored* Jessica and always tried to imitate her. For instance, on her last visit, she had insisted on buying some clothes like Jessica's, and she looked so bad in them that Jessica could barely stand to wear them again. Jessica certainly hoped this wouldn't happen again.

"Where'd you ever find that gorgeous sweater?" Jenny asked, her eyes shining behind her thick glasses.

Jessica grimaced. "Oh, I forget," she said quickly, trying not to meet her sister's accusing stare.

"I'm on a diet," Jenny announced cheerfully. "I've made up my mind, just looking at you two. I want to be thin, too!"

"You look fine just the way you are, Jen," Elizabeth said immediately.

Jessica stared at her. Elizabeth, she thought, was losing either her eyesight or her judgment!

"Jenny, I put your things upstairs," Mr.

Wakefield said, popping his head into the living room. "In Jessica's room. Is that all right?"

"All right! It's *perfect*," Jenny shrieked. "Just think, Jess, we can stay up all night talking."

"Uh—that sounds great," Jessica said weakly, backing down under her father's stare.

Secretly she couldn't imagine anything she'd rather *not* do than stay up all night, listening to Jenny. Elizabeth had urged her to keep an open mind until their cousin actually arrived. Well, Jenny was there now, and for once Jessica had to admit Elizabeth was right in one respect. Jenny *wasn't* as bad as she had expected—she was worse! A thousand times worse! And *Jessica* was the one who was going to be stuck with her most of the time.

"Lila, how much longer do we have to stay here?" Jessica demanded in a low voice. She and Lila were sitting in a crowded booth at Casey's Place, a popular ice-cream parlor.

That afternoon Lila had overheard Aaron say that he and Jeffrey were going to be at Casey's that night. Lila had convinced Jessica to go to Casey's with her. At the moment they were sharing a booth with Eddie Winters and Ken Matthews. Even though Jessica would normally have been ecstatic about running into Eddie, she couldn't help wishing that Aaron and Jeffrey would show up soon. Although Jessica never cared whether or not she was late, she *hated* to wait for anyone else. To make everything worse, Jenny had insisted on coming along. Her elbow kept jabbing Jessica's side, and she was getting ice cream all over everything. Jessica looked at her with distaste. She couldn't believe Jenny was eating an enormous banana split less than an hour after the huge dinner Mrs. Wakefield had prepared. No wonder her figure was such a mess! What had happened to her resolve to diet?

"Want some?" Jenny offered, holding a spoonful of ice cream in front of Jessica. A melted drop landed on the table.

Jessica flinched. "No, thanks," she said acidly. Jenny was much worse than she had remembered. The girl was such a bookworm! She had even brought some stupid novel with her to Casey's, which was the most ridiculous thing Jessica had ever heard of. With her thick glasses and silly smile, Jenny was truly pitiable. But any feeling of pity Jessica might have had ended the minute Jenny spoke. The girl had no shame! Jessica thought. She had no idea she was the biggest nerd in the world. For instance, when Ken Matthews asked her what book she was reading, she had actually launched into a whole boring account of the author's life! Jessica had been mortified—especially since Eddie was sitting across from them listening to the whole thing.

Even worse, Jenny hung on Jessica's every word and made it sound as if the two of them were best friends. It made Jessica cringe. The only salvageable part of the evening was getting to stare at Eddie. Jessica made her mind up then and there that he was the guy for her, even though he didn't look like the type she usually went for. He was tall and thin, with reddish-brown hair and a spattering of freckles across his nose. He seemed to be shy, too. But his smile just made her melt! He was such a gentleman. He didn't even ridicule Jenny when she went on and on about those boring authors of hers. In fact he went so far as to *talk* to her about them! Jessica couldn't believe what a find Eddie was. If only Jenny would get lost so she herself could spend some time alone with him!

Suddenly Lila jumped up from the booth and waved her arms excitedly. "Aaron!" she called. "Jeffrey! Come and join us!"

At last, Jessica thought grumpily.

"Hi, everyone," Aaron said, coming over to the booth. He looked questioningly at Jenny, and Jessica introduced them.

"And this is Jeffrey French. I think you've met almost everyone here," Aaron said.

"Yes," Lila cooed, staring meaningfully at Jeffrey. "Jeffrey and I are *old* friends, aren't we?"

"It looks a little crowded here, Lila," Aaron said doubtfully, looking at the booth.

"Oh, *no* it isn't. It isn't crowded at all!" Lila exclaimed, moving sideways into Eddie. "Jeffrey, there's plenty of room here," she added emphatically, patting the space beside her. Jeffrey stared at her, his face reddening. Jessica rolled her eyes, wishing she and Eddie were out on the beach, alone, instead of smashed in here with all these people. Jenny was starting in on foreign movies now, as if books weren't bad enough, asking Eddie which ones he had seen.

"Jess, can I squeeze in?" Aaron asked apologetically. Three people could fit on each side of the booth, but four was a very tight fit.

"Why not?" Jessica said unhappily. They all moved over as far as they could, and Jessica realized, with an inward groan, that she was now stuck at the part of the table that was all sticky with ice cream.

"Jeffrey," Lila said, her brown eyes wide with feigned admiration, "I hear you're from a farm in Oregon. Is that true?"

Jeffrey smiled. "As a matter of fact, yes. Why? Are you interested in farms?"

Jessica snorted, averting her eyes to avoid Lila's cold glare.

"As a matter of fact, I am," Lila purred, slipping her hand closer to his on the table. Within minutes she was telling him all about her predicament with the horse her father wanted to buy her.

"Well, I don't really know much about horses," Jeffrey admitted. "My father ran a timber farm in Oregon. I'm afraid we really didn't have very many animals, just a lot of trees."

Lila's hand inched even closer. "I love the out-of-doors," she said rapturously. "I bet you really like to swim," she added.

Jeffrey blinked. "Swimming's all right. I'm better at soccer, but, sure, I like swimming."

"Oh, *good*," Lila said. "Then you can come to the pool party I'm having tomorrow!"

Jessica resisted the urge to giggle. Lila's spontaneous parties had become legendary at Sweet Valley High, and they were almost always organized when Lila had her eye on some guy. Apparently this was to be no exception.

From Jessica's point of view, it was hard to tell whether or not Jeffrey was responding to Lila. He seemed like an amazingly nice guy, friendly, open, easygoing. He was even better looking up close than Jessica had realized. He had thick, shiny blond hair and wonderful green eyes. Everything about him seemed casual and relaxed, from his cotton, button-down shirt, rolled up at the sleeves, to his slightly scuffed loafers. "I'd love to come," he said to Lila, his smile including the others at the table—even Jenny. "I've really been looking forward to meeting more people from school. Will there be lots of people there?"

"Oh, just a few," Lila murmured, her fingers brushing his as if by accident.

"I love pool parties," Jenny chimed in, her brown eyes shining behind her glasses. "Can I come?"

Lila looked helplessly at Jessica, who shook her head in despair.

"Of course," Lila said tersely, turning back to Jeffrey. "Everyone's invited."

"We'll talk about it later," Jessica hissed, hoping Eddie hadn't heard her. The last thing she wanted was for Jenny to follow her everywhere for the next two weeks.

But she couldn't see any way around it. If Lila wanted to have one of her famous parties, Lila was going to do it. And it looked as though once again Jenny would be there to ruin Jessica's day.

"Eddie's so nice," Jenny said enthusiastically. She and Jessica were on their way home from Casey's, and Jessica was trying to concentrate on the road.

Jessica tried to keep her temper. "Jenny—" she began.

But her cousin was staring at her with her usual admiring smile. "I think he's cuter than Jeffrey French. Don't you?"

Jessica thought this over. "In a different way, I guess."

"Well, I think he's cuter." Jenny wrinkled her nose. "I can't believe everyone thinks Jeffrey's so great! Who do you think he likes better," she added curiously, "Enid or Lila?"

"*Enid*?" Jessica demanded, horrified. "Why would he like *Enid*?"

Jenny's brown eyes widened. "Well, I thought Liz was trying to help Enid get together with him. I heard—" She broke off when she saw the expression on Jessica's face. "Uh-oh," she said, slapping her hand over her mouth. "Did I say something wrong?"

"No, Jen," Jessica said grimly. "What did you hear?"

Jenny looked uncomfortable. "Well, I acciden-

29

tally overheard Liz talking to Enid on the phone after dinner. And she kept encouraging Enid, saying that she was a million times better suited to Jeffrey than Lila."

"Oh, she did, did she?" Jessica seethed. So *that* was Elizabeth's plan! Well, it wasn't going to work. Did Elizabeth really believe for a minute that she could outfox her own twin? Suddenly Jessica's desire to match up Lila and Jeffrey was doubled. There was no way she would let Elizabeth outmaneuver her!

The next minute Jessica remembered Lila's pool party. *All's fair in love and war*, she reminded herself. And it seemed only fair to exclude Enid and Elizabeth from the guest list!

"Listen, Jen," Jessica said carefully. "I have to ask you a bit of a favor about tomorrow. Liz probably wouldn't want to come anyway, but would you mind not telling her about it?"

"Why shouldn't I?" Jenny demanded.

Jessica thought fast. She felt uncomfortable, interfering with Elizabeth's plans, but she couldn't stomach the thought of someone as cute as Jeffrey being wasted on someone as dull as Enid Rollings. No, Jeffrey was much better off with Lila. Lila might have her problems, but she sure wasn't dull.

"Well," Jessica said, trying desperately to

think of a good white lie, "Lila and Liz really don't get along. I mean, Lila really doesn't like Liz, and no matter what I say to her, she just won't invite her to anything! You can imagine how much it would hurt Liz's feelings to hear there was a party and she didn't get invited. So let's just keep it a secret, OK?"

"OK," Jenny said, staring at Jessica with rapt admiration.

Jessica sighed. She had her work cut out for her, trying to keep Elizabeth and Enid away from Jeffrey French. And on top of that, she had to make a move fast, or Eddie was going to lose interest.

Jessica just couldn't believe her rotten luck. Why in the world had her bratty little cousin chosen to descend on them just when she and Eddie were on the verge of falling madly in love?

Three

"Jess, this isn't working," Lila moaned, surveying the scene before her with complete exasperation. As usual, the Fowler estate was immaculate. The lush grounds were perfectly manicured, and the enormous pool sparkled in the sunlight. At either end of the pool, tables were set up, laden with cold drinks and salads. Hamburgers were sizzling on the barbecue grill, and music was wafting out from the outdoor speakers near the cabana. All the ingredients were there for a perfect afternoon, but Jessica knew that Lila took all this for granted. Sneaking a little glance at her friend out of the corner of her eye, Jessica had to admit Lila had taken special pains with her appearance. She was wearing a sleek, one-piece bathing suit—black, with a white band around it that showed off her golden tan—and a white sarong slung casually around her hips. Her light brown hair was tied up in a sleek bun at the nape of her neck, and the total effect was both exotic and sexy.

But Jessica could see what Lila meant; Jeffrey hadn't been paying much attention to his hostess. Not that he wasn't perfectly charming and friendly. He said all the right things, but it was obvious he wanted to get to know Lila's other guests, too. In fact he had gone so far as to suggest a game of water volleyball, and right now was deep in the fray. Eddie was captain of one team and Jeffrey of another, and from the excited shouts and laughter coming from the pool, the game was apparently a big success.

"I wish they'd all get out of there," Lila fumed, adjusting her sarong. "How am I supposed to get to know Jeffrey if he's going to spend the whole day thrashing around with that stupid ball?"

Jessica giggled. "Liz warned you that he's the athletic type, remember?"

Lila's eyes flashed. "I went to all this trouble just for him, and he doesn't even appreciate it."

Jessica shook her head. "Remember, he thinks

this party was arranged ages ago. Give him a chance, Lila. Besides, he looks so wonderful in a bathing suit. What a body!"

"Yes," Lila said and sighed, "he sure does. Well, maybe I can get everyone out of the pool by saying that lunch is ready."

Jessica couldn't help agreeing that she wished the water volleyball match would end soon. After all, *she* wasn't getting to spend any time with Eddie, either. The game did have one advantage, however: Jenny liked to swim, and at least the game was keeping her little cousin out of her hair!

Jessica sank down into a lounge chair, crossing her long legs at the ankles and pretending to watch the game while she waited for Lila to announce it was time to eat. She knew she looked good and hoped Eddie would be distracted enough to jump out of the water and join her. Jessica's tiny bikini left little to the imagination. Unlike Lila's, her own hair was loose around her shoulders, glinting in the sunlight. She felt so good, lying in the sun. . . . Within seconds Jessica was in a deep reverie, imagining how spectacular it would be the first time she and Eddie kissed. She was absorbed in her daydream when icy water dripping on her legs made her jump up with a little cry. It was Jenny, riding on Eddie's shoulders, dribbling cold water on her cousin and smiling triumphantly.

"We won!" Jenny cried out as Eddie leaned over to set her down on the pavement.

Jessica glared at her, then grabbed her towel to brush the offending drops from her legs. "That's great," she snapped. She couldn't believe Eddie was carrying on this way. It was one thing being nice to the poor child. But giving her a piggyback ride was overdoing it.

"We came over to see if you wanted to eat with us," Eddie said, giving her a smile that made her anger melt.

"Sure," Jessica said, swinging her legs around and smiling up at him from lowered lashes. Only one thing kept her from being overjoyed at the prospect.

Why did Jenny have to be there? If it weren't for her pain-in-the-neck cousin, she and Eddie could have a romantic little lunch under the big shade trees.

If ever there had been a case of two's company, three's a crowd, it seemed to Jessica that this was it!

"Hi, Jen," Elizabeth said conversationally, joining her cousin in the Wakefields' sunny,

Spanish-tiled kitchen. It was early Sunday morning, and the house was quiet. Jessica was still asleep, and Mr. and Mrs. Wakefield were out, running errands. "You're an early bird this morning! Can I get you some orange juice?"

"Sure," Jenny said, putting a bookmark in the novel she was reading. "Liz, I'm having such a good time out here! I wish I could stay in California all the time with you and Jessica!"

Elizabeth smiled as she poured two glasses of orange juice. She could think of one person who wouldn't be overjoyed if *that* wish ever came true.

"Well, it must be fun living in Dallas," she remarked as she brought the glasses to the table.

"Not as much fun as it is here," Jenny said. "I had such a good time yesterday." She paused for a moment, then asked, "Don't you think Eddie Winters is the cutest guy in the whole world?"

Elizabeth smiled. "He *is* cute," she said. She looked curiously at her cousin's glowing face. "Where did you see Eddie?" she asked casually. Elizabeth had spent most of the previous day at Enid's house. She hadn't seen Jessica at all, and she wondered now whether Jessica could possibly have brought Jenny along with her on a date with Eddie.

"Oh, just around," Jenny said, looking

instantly guilty. "He's going to take Jessica and me out this Friday night," she added, taking a big sip of orange juice.

"That should be fun," Elizabeth said. *Jessica must be furious*, she thought as she pulled a chair up across from her cousin. Her first real date with Eddie, and Jessica would have to share it with her least favorite relative!

"He's so strong and everything," Jenny went on, her eyes dreamy. "And he likes reading, too!"

"Really," Elizabeth said absently, glancing at the magazine section of the Sunday paper.

"You should've seen him yesterday." Jenny giggled. "We were having this volleyball game in the pool, and it was the final point—Jeffrey's team was winning—and he made this incredible leap across the whole pool and saved it!"

Elizabeth stared at her cousin. "Jeffrey?" she repeated blankly. "Jenny, where was this volleyball game taking place?"

Jenny's face turned crimson. "Uh—oh no, I've done it again," she said miserably. "I *always* do dumb things like this!"

"Jenny Townsend," Elizabeth said grimly, "you'd better tell me what's going on!"

"But Jessica said I shouldn't," Jenny whispered, chagrined.

Elizabeth's eyes flashed. "Tell me," she insisted firmly.

"She just didn't want your feelings to be hurt," Jenny protested, her eyes round with fear. "Honestly, Liz. She told me that Lila never invites you to her parties, and she said it would just make you feel bad if—"

"Jenny," Elizabeth said, fighting for control, "just tell me one thing. Was Jeffrey French at Lila's party yesterday?"

Jenny nodded.

"It figures," Elizabeth said angrily. One look at her cousin's face convinced her to change her tone. "Don't worry about it, Jen," she said, patting her cousin's arm. "You haven't done anything wrong. And I'm not mad at you. Honestly!"

"Then you won't tell Jessica that I told you?" Jenny begged.

Elizabeth sighed. "I guess not," she said. She didn't want to get poor Jenny in more trouble with Jessica. *I can't believe that girl*, she thought. Of all the rotten tricks! Jessica and Lila had clearly planned the party in the hope of getting Lila and Jeffrey together. It was too coincidental that Enid and Elizabeth had just been accidentally left off the guest list!

After she had breakfast, Elizabeth excused

herself and went up to her room to get dressed. As she was getting ready, the phone rang and she picked up her extension.

"Liz," Enid moaned into the phone, her voice anguished, "I just got a call from Olivia, and she told me Lila had a pool party yesterday and was throwing herself all over Jeffrey!"

"I know," Elizabeth said grimly. "I just got a report from my cousin Jenny. I could kill Jessica. She must've been in on the whole thing!"

Enid sounded hysterical. "Liz, if Jessica is on Lila's side, we don't stand a chance! She always gets her way when it comes to things like this!"

Elizabeth's eyes flashed. "Not this time," she vowed. "I'm not kidding, Enid. I'm really mad. And I'm not going to sit back and let her do this to us! You and I have got to start fighting fire with fire."

Enid was quiet for a minute. "Did Jenny say whether or not Jeffrey and Lila spent a lot of time together?" she asked in a low voice.

"I didn't get a chance to ask her," Elizabeth admitted. "But I'm not going to let you give up yet, Enid."

"What are we going to *do*?" Enid wailed.

"Enid," Elizabeth said, a thought occurring to her, "isn't there a volleyball game in the gym tomorrow night?"

"Yes," Enid said. "I think we're playing Parker High. Why?"

"I want you to go to that game," Elizabeth said, her eyes beginning to sparkle. "And make sure you save a place on the bleachers for Jeffrey. I'll find a way to convince him he needs to get involved in school activities right away if he wants to be a good photographer for the paper. And tomorrow night looks like as good a time as any for him to get started!"

"I hope it works," Enid said. "I never would have guessed it, but it looks like you may be worthy competition for Jessica after all!"

Elizabeth laughed. She was thinking that it was high time *Jessica* realized that. With any luck, the next couple of days would demonstrate that Jessica wasn't the only Wakefield twin capable of serious matchmaking!

It was Sunday afternoon, and Jessica was just on her way out to the pool, when the Wakefields' front door bell rang.

"Eddie!" Jessica exclaimed as she opened the front door. "Come on in! What brings you here on such a gorgeous Sunday afternoon?"

Running his hand through his tousled hair,

Eddie smiled shyly and said, "I just hoped I could—"

"Eddie!" Jenny called from the staircase. Jessica's heart fell. She couldn't believe it. Eddie Winters had finally summoned up his courage to drop by, and Jenny, once again, was going to force herself between them.

Jessica still couldn't believe the events of the day before. It wasn't that she hadn't had fun at Lila's party, it was just that Jenny had been constantly in the way. Every time she and Eddie had tried to start a conversation, Jenny was right in the middle of it, yakking about those god-awful books she was so big on. It had been awful. The crowning humiliation had come when Eddie mentioned something about that coming Friday night, and Jenny, like a moron, just *assumed* she would be included. Jessica couldn't believe Eddie was stoic enough to put up with this farcical situation. She just hoped Jenny didn't get on his nerves so much that he decided to forget completely about Jessica!

She and Lila had spent the whole evening before commiserating. Lila felt depressed about Jeffrey. Not that he hadn't had fun—he had made it clear that the party had been the best thing to happen to him since his family moved to Sweet Valley. But he hadn't paid much attention to Lila. He divided his time equally among the guests, trying as hard as possible to get to know each one of them. He even spent a long time talking to Jenny! Jessica couldn't blame Lila for feeling low about the whole thing, but they had agreed they would just have to redouble their efforts the coming week. Jessica was sure Enid would give up as soon as she realized just how badly Lila wanted Jeffrey. Not even Enid Rollins could be moronic enough to try to compete with Lila Fowler!

"Why don't we go out to the pool?" Jessica suggested, looking meaningfully at Eddie.

"Great. Let me just put my book away!" Jenny exclaimed.

Jessica glared at her. "Maybe you should stay inside and finish it," she suggested, hoping Jenny would take the hint. Jenny just stared at her, completely crestfallen.

"Oh, come outside with us," Eddie said, smiling sympathetically at the girl. "It's too nice a day to be indoors."

Jessica couldn't believe her ears. Eddie Winters was the nicest boy in the whole world! *I really am lucky*, she told herself as she led the way out to the patio and the Wakefields' swimming pool. *He must be incredibly patient to put up with Jenny Townsend for two days running!*

But as the afternoon dragged on, Jessica's own patience began to wear thin. Eddie stayed for over an hour, and Jenny stayed right beside them the entire time. She seemed oblivious to the fact that Jessica wanted to be alone with Eddie. None of the hints Jessica dropped worked, either. Finally Eddie said he'd have to be going—and Jenny followed Jessica out to the car while they said goodbye. Jessica had had it. She bounded up the short flight of stairs to the second floor of the house. It was high time to tell her mother the misery she'd been put through!

"Mom, I've had it," Jessica seethed, closing the door to her parents' bedroom behind her. Mrs. Wakefield was applying makeup, getting ready for a dinner party she and Mr. Wakefield had been invited to.

"Had it with what?" she asked, giving her daughter a smile. "Which do you thinks looks better, the pearl pin or this silver one?"

Jessica frowned. "They both look fine," she said grouchily. The truth was that Mrs. Wakefield looked beautiful. Still slender enough to trade clothes with the twins, Alice Wakefield was often teased about looking like the girls' older sister. Her soft blond hair framed her face perfectly, and her eyes looked even bluer lately because of her tan. "Oh, I guess the pearl pin," Jessica said at last.

"Thanks," her mother said, smiling. "Now, what's up?"

"Jenny," Jessica groaned. "The girl is driving me out of my mind! Mother, she follows me around like a shadow! Can't I tell her to get lost—to leave me alone even for just an hour?"

"The girl, as you put it, happens to be your first cousin—and my sister's daughter," Mrs. Wakefield said reprovingly. "Not only that, she's a guest in our house, and as long as she's here, you owe it to her to be a good hostess. You may *not* tell her to get lost—under any circumstances."

"But, Mom—"

"No 'buts,' " Mrs. Wakefield said firmly. "I'm not kidding, Jess. I don't want to hear another complaint about her. Do you understand?"

Jessica's eyes welled with tears. She understood, all right. She understood that she was going to have another ten days of torture.

She just didn't know whether she was going to be able to stand it!

Four

Elizabeth was sitting at her desk in the *Oracle* office, looking over what she had written about the PTA Food-Drive Week. "I'm so glad Sweet Valley High has a food drive every year," she remarked to Penny Ayala, the editor of the paper. "It's hard to believe there are people in our own town who don't have enough to eat!"

"I know," Penny said soberly. "And it seems so simple, too, once it's all been organized. I think the auction's going to be great this year."

"Me, too," Elizabeth agreed. *The Oracle*'s special supplement on the drive highlighted the auction that would take place the following Friday and the beach party on Sunday for all participants. Elizabeth was covering the auction. She was delighted with the assignment, too. It seemed to Elizabeth that the auction would be the highlight of the week-long drive. The auction was run by the school committee, headed this year by Enid Rollins, and the idea was for students to come up with things to auction off, using canned food rather than money to make the bids. In past years students had brought incredibly funny and imaginative things to auction off, and Elizabeth was sure this year's auction would be every bit as lively, especially since Winston Egbert, the acknowledged clown of the junior class, had volunteered to be the auctioneer.

"Hi, girls," Mr. Collins called, coming into the office and setting down a pile of papers. "How's it going?"

Elizabeth grinned. "Don't tell me you're planning on auctioning off our English papers," she joked.

Roger Collins chuckled. "I'm not sure I'd get more than a single can of soup for the whole lot," he teased. The strawberry-blond English teacher was extremely popular. He was always ready to listen to a student's problem, or crack a joke or two in the hallway. Elizabeth had gotten to know Mr. Collins, both in her English class and from her work on *The Oracle*, as he was the paper's faculty adviser.

"Say, has Jeffrey French stopped by the office?" Mr. Collins asked, checking his watch. "Have you two met him yet? He's the new boy from Oregon."

"I know who he is," Elizabeth said casually, "but he hasn't come by the office. Why? Is he supposed to pick something up?"

"Darn," Mr. Collins said. "I've got to take off soon to pick Teddy up from the baby-sitter's." Teddy, Mr. Collins's six-year-old son, had been left in his father's custody when the Collinses' marriage ended in divorce. "Penny, are you going to be around for a while?" Mr. Collins asked.

Penny shook her head. "I've got to go over to the printer's to talk about the supplement. Unless you really need me to stay here for some reason," she added.

"I'll be here," Elizabeth said. "Can I help?"

"Well, maybe you can. Would you mind showing Jeffrey around the place and letting him know what sort of help we need to finish up the supplement?"

"Sure!" Elizabeth said. What a stroke of luck! she thought happily. She would be able to talk to

Jeffrey and there wouldn't be anyone else to interfere.

"That's great, Liz," Penny said, looking relieved. "If you really don't mind, I think I'm going to leave now. Is that OK?"

Elizabeth laughed, making little shooing motions with her hands. "Go on, both of you!" she said lightly.

"Well, I guess I might as well see you out, Penny," Mr. Collins conceded. Several minutes later they had gathered their things, said goodbye to Elizabeth, and closed the office door behind them. Elizabeth breathed a sigh of relief. The more she thought about it, the more she realized that she actually had a pretty big order to fill for Enid. Elizabeth didn't have a lot of experience fixing people up with each other, and she didn't know Jeffrey French very well. Did she have any right to promise her friend that everything would work out between them?

Elizabeth's reverie was interrupted by a knock on the door. "Come in!" she said, her voice sounding strange in the silent office.

"Hello," Jeffrey said, smiling at her. "Hey, I didn't know *you* worked for the paper!"

Elizabeth smiled. "You may be mixing me up with Jessica, my twin sister," she told him. "Don't worry, it happens all the time," she assured him when he looked embarrassed. "I met you when you came over to our house with Aaron a little over a week ago. Remember? I'm Elizabeth."

"Oh, yes," Jeffrey said. He looked at her so carefully that it was Elizabeth's turn to feel embarrassed. "Come to think of it, I can't believe I made that mistake. You two really are completely different, aren' t you?"

Elizabeth smiled quizzically at him. "Well, we *are* twins," she pointed out. "What do you mean, 'completely different'?"

Jeffrey shrugged. "I don't know. You seem quieter, a little more serious." He gazed at her, then said, "I bet it's kind of hard being a twin." There was a question in his voice.

Elizabeth laughed. "Well, it's hard at times. But Jessica's a lot of fun. I don't think I'll trade her in yet."

Jeffrey laughed and took a seat next to Elizabeth's desk. "Sorry. There I go, getting ahead of myself again. I guess I can be a little *too* direct at times. And I didn't come here to analyze you and your sister, either. I came to find out what I could do to help with the paper."

Elizabeth nodded. "Mr. Collins told me you'd be coming by. He had to leave early today, so he asked me to make a few suggestions for you. Is that all right?''

''More than all right,'' Jeffrey said, his green eyes warm.

Elizabeth blushed. ''Uh—you're a photographer, aren't you?'' she asked, trying to keep her self-control. Something about the way Jeffrey was looking at her was unnerving. She couldn't pinpoint the way it made her feel. She just knew she felt uneasy.

''Yep,'' Jeffrey said. ''I worked for my school paper in Oregon for the last two years. But I like taking pictures of things outside of school, too. You know, a paper can get a little routine—you usually end up shooting a dance or a game. I'm pretty dedicated when it comes to photography. I wouldn't mind turning it into a career one day.''

Elizabeth stared at him. ''I know how you feel. I feel that way about writing, too. Not that I don't like writing the 'Eyes and Ears' column, but I hope to write seriously. This is really just a beginning.''

''The 'Eyes and Ears' column?'' Jeffrey asked curiously. ''What's that?''

Elizabeth smiled. ''It's the gossip column, as a matter of fact. And it keeps me pretty busy around here, I can tell you that much!''

"I'll bet," Jeffrey said, looking at her with the same searching, curious gaze. "I bet a girl like you is pretty busy all the time," he added softly. "For example, I bet you've got a boyfriend, right?"

Elizabeth's cheeks burned. "Uh—no, as a matter of fact, I don't," she said quickly. This wasn't the way she had planned the conversation at all! Taking a deep breath, Elizabeth changed the subject. As matter of factly as possible, she began to explain what *The Oracle* would be doing for the next few weeks and how she thought Jeffrey could get involved. He listened attentively and asked several good questions, and within minutes Elizabeth felt at ease. Soon they were joking and laughing like old friends, trading silly anecdotes about working on a school paper. Jeffrey was also telling Elizabeth about soccer, which he loved. Before she knew it, it was five-thirty, and she hadn't even broached the subject of Enid or the game!

"Listen, Jeffrey, have you gotten to know very many people at school yet?" she asked conversationally.

Jeffrey shook his head. "Not many, but I'm trying to remedy that. It takes a little time, I guess, but being on the soccer team will help. I think before long I'll feel OK here."

"You know, I have a friend you should get to know," Elizabeth told him. "Her name is Enid Rollins. You met her at the party at my house. She's a wonderful girl, though of course I may just be biased, since she's my best friend. Do you remember her?" Elizabeth continued uneasily. "She's got curly brown hair and green eyes."

"Oh, sure," Jeffrey said lightly. "I'd like to get to know all of your friends." He reached for his jacket. "Hey, why don't you let me give you a ride home, and you can give me a guided tour of the neighborhood?"

Elizabeth laughed. "Sorry, but I drove today, too. Enid is the one who ought to be giving you guided tours, anyway," she confided, putting on her cardigan. "The girl knows more about Sweet Valley than anyone I can think of. I'm not kidding, Jeffrey. You really have to get to know her."

As Jeffrey scooped his books up, he looked thoughtfully at Elizabeth. "Why don't the three of us get together, then?"

Elizabeth thought fast. "I've got a wonderful idea," she said quickly. "Are you going to the volleyball game tonight?"

Jeffrey shook his head. "I hadn't planned on it. Why? Are you going to be there?"

Elizabeth pretended to think it over. "Well, I'd

like to, but my cousin is visiting us from Texas, and I promised my mother I'd do something with her tonight. But that means I can't go to the game with Enid like I promised. Maybe you could do me a big favor and take my place."

Jeffrey opened the door for Elizabeth as they left the office together. "That sounds like fun," he said noncommittally. "But why don't you bring your cousin to the game, and we can all go together?"

"Well, I think Jenny might have something else in mind," Elizabeth fibbed. "But, honestly, Jeffrey, it would be a really good idea for you to go. You'll meet some great people, and it probably wouldn't hurt to take a few pictures of the game. We've got our regular photographer in charge, but he could always use a little help."

"Sounds like a good idea," Jeffrey said lightly. They walked down the hall together in companionable silence, and Elizabeth noticed, almost despite herself, how tall and well built he was. *Enid's right*, she thought appreciatively. *He really is cute.*

"But that still doesn't settle one thing," Jeffrey added. "When are you going to find time to give me that tour of Sweet Valley?"

Elizabeth laughed. "You know where to find

me," she reminded him. "For the next week or two, I won't be budging from the *Oracle* office."

"Hey," Jeffrey said suddenly, as they opened the main doors and strolled outside the building. "I don't suppose you have time to stop at Casey's and have a Coke, do you?"

Elizabeth thought for a minute. Actually, she *did* have time. She was thirsty, too, and she really wouldn't mind getting to know Jeffrey a little better.

But somehow it didn't seem right. "I wish I could," Elizabeth said. "But I really have to get home and keep Jenny company. My sister," she added with a rueful laugh, "has been working overtime in that department, and she's not too happy about that!"

"Well, maybe some other time," Jeffrey said.

Elizabeth had the distinct impression he was disappointed. *But why?* she asked herself. That uneasy feeling was back again, but Elizabeth pushed it away. "Listen, about tonight," she said again. "Look for Enid if you go to the game. You really should get to know her better," she added pointedly.

Jeffrey looked at her quizzically. "I'll do my best," he said at last. "Well, here's my car," he added, stopping at a small, repainted sports car with a convertible top. "Thanks for showing me around the office, Liz."

Elizabeth watched him get into the car, her expression thoughtful. She couldn't kid herself. Jeffrey didn't seem very excited at the prospect of getting together with Enid. All she could do was hope that he'd make it that night. Because she knew if he didn't, Enid was going to be very disappointed.

Five

Twenty minutes later Elizabeth was sitting on the edge of Enid's bed, watching her friend get dressed. "Remember, he didn't say he could definitely come," Elizabeth warned.

"Oh, Liz, you're the best friend ever!" Enid had shrieked when Elizabeth told her that she had suggested to Jeffrey that he try to find Enid at the game. For the past few minutes Enid had been running around her room in a frenzy, yanking clothes out of one drawer after another, pulling a hairbrush through her hair, knocking perfume bottles over in her excitement. "Tell me what happened," she begged as she slipped into a blue sweater. "Tell me *everything*."

"Well," Elizabeth said, thinking, "you're absolutely right—he's wonderful. He seems really down-to-earth. He's interested in tons of things—photography, journalism, sports. . . . He's a really nice guy!"

Enid stared at her friend. "What's wrong?" she demanded.

"Nothing," Elizabeth said, forcing a laugh. "Why should anything be wrong?"

She couldn't tell Enid that she felt peculiar about the conversation she and Jeffrey had had. Elizabeth had never tried blatantly to fix anyone up, and it was extremely embarrassing. She had always thought that people were smart enough to figure out who they were interested in on their own. But she had promised Enid, and Enid was her best friend.

"Anyway, I sure can't see him with Lila," Elizabeth said, trying to brush away her slightly guilty feeling. "Lila seems the last girl in the world Jeffrey would ever like."

"I hope you're right," Enid said, brushing her hair until it shone. "How do I look, Liz?"

Elizabeth jumped up to give her friend an impulsive hug. "You look wonderful," she said sincerely. "Jeffrey French would have to be out of his mind not to think you're the prettiest girl in the bleachers tonight!"

"Liz, I just don't know how to thank you—" Enid began.

"Don't," Elizabeth interrupted with a laugh. "Or at least wait and thank me after you two get together! I'd better run," she added reluctantly. "Jessica and Jenny will probably have killed each other by the time I get home."

She couldn't help wondering what was going to happen that night. Would Jeffrey actually go along to the game and find Enid?

Elizabeth hoped so. Or at least she thought she did. It was terrible, but one tiny part of her seemed to hope that he *wouldn't*. Only she didn't have the faintest idea why she felt that way.

"Oh, Liz, it was awful," Enid gushed into the phone. It was ten o'clock, and Elizabeth was curled up in front of the television set in the den, her journal lying beside her on the couch. She hadn't been able to concentrate on anything that evening, and when the phone rang, she realized that unconsciously she had been waiting for Enid to call.

"What do you mean?" Elizabeth demanded. "He didn't show up?"

Enid seemed to be close to tears. "No. I sat there and waited through the whole game, but no Jeffrey French. Liz, I feel like the biggest idiot in the whole world."

"Enid," Elizabeth said, her heart filling with sympathy, "you can't let it get to you! He must've had something that kept him from coming. You know what it's like when you first move to a new place. He probably has to help his parents with things around the new house."

"I doubt it," Enid said miserably. "He probably just doesn't want to have anything to do with me."

"Enid, you can't talk this way," Elizabeth said fiercely. "For heaven's sake, he doesn't even know you yet!"

"Well, that's true," Enid admitted. "Unless he thinks I'm really hideous," she said a split second later.

"Enid," Elizabeth said warningly. "Now, look. The whole point is for you to find some way to get a chance to talk to Jeffrey to see whether or not you two get along with each other. Until that happens you can't blame him for seeming reluctant. Maybe he's shy. Maybe he doesn't like the thought of approaching you on his own."

Enid began to sound slightly less desperate. "Do you think so, Liz? Did he really seem the slightest bit interested this afternoon, or were you just trying to make me feel better?"

"He definitely seemed interested," Elizabeth said. She knew she wasn't exactly telling the truth, but she couldn't bear the thought of hurting Enid's feelings. "Uh-oh. I think Jenny and Jessica are home. I'd better find out where they've been," Elizabeth said hastily. Mrs. Wakefield had been concerned about Jenny and Jessica, who had disappeared after dinner without mentioning where they were going.

"Liz, thanks for everything," Enid said.

"Don't lose heart!" Elizabeth said before hanging up the phone.

Picking up her journal, Liz walked out into the hallway and saw Jenny.

"Hi, Liz!" Jenny sang out, slipping out of her coat and coming over to where Elizabeth was standing. Jenny's face was flushed with excitement. "You'll never guess where I've been."

"I bet you've been somewhere with Jessica," Elizabeth replied.

"That's right," Jenny said happily. "We went dancing with a whole bunch of people at the Beach Disco. And Eddie Winters danced with me *three* times," she added.

Elizabeth resisted the impulse to laugh. *I bet Jessica really got a kick out of that*, she thought.

Actually she couldn't help noticing how much prettier Jenny looked that night. It must have been the excitement, or the glow she had gotten from dancing, Elizabeth thought. But she really did look sweet, almost like a different person.

"Who else went?" Elizabeth asked casually.

"Lila and Jessica and Eddie," Jenny said, ticking off fingers with each name. "And Jeffrey French, and Roger and Olivia. We met some other people there, too."

"Jeffrey—" Elizabeth started. "Jeffrey was there?" she demanded.

Jenny nodded. "It was so romantic," she said rapturously. "He and Lila kept dancing together to all these slow songs. You could just tell from the way they were holding each other that they were falling madly in love."

Elizabeth's face burned. So that was why he hadn't met Enid at the volleyball game! She couldn't believe he'd do a rotten thing like that to poor Enid. The more she thought about it, the angrier she felt. "Are you sure they were dancing together?" she asked.

Jenny blinked. "Of course I'm sure," she said. "Lila's nuts about him, Liz. She's getting tickets to some big professional soccer game so she can ask him to it. And she's going to ask her father to give her an advance on her allowance so she can buy him a new camera."

Elizabeth's heart began to pound. She couldn't stand the thought of Lila and Jeffrey slow-dancing together. It seemed—well, it seemed so unfair!

Suddenly Elizabeth didn't want to be down-stairs when Jessica came inside and gave her own account of the budding romance between Jeffrey and Lila. Saying a quick good-night to Jenny, Elizabeth hurried toward the stairs.

She wasn't sure why she was so upset about the whole thing, but she assured herself any good friend would feel the way she was feeling.

She didn't even answer Jenny, who was call-ing after her. Elizabeth didn't feel like talking to anyone; she just wanted to be alone.

"Hey, Jess?" Jenny said sleepily. She was curled up on the cot in Jessica's room in her nightgown, a paperback open in her hand.

"What?" Jessica said grouchily, turning the volume down on her Walkman. She was in the middle of doing leg lifts and didn't want to be interrupted. It was just too unbearable having to share a room with Jenny.

"I was just wondering what we're going to do with Eddie Friday night," Jenny said dreamily.

Jessica sat up and looked at her cousin with a mixture of fury and contempt. "I don't know, Jen. What do *you* feel like doing?" she asked sarcastically.

But sarcasm was wasted on Jenny Townsend. "I'm so glad you asked!" she exclaimed. "There's a wonderful old movie on at the Plaza— *Wuthering Heights*. I just know Eddie would love it."

Jessica tried to control herself, but it was getting harder and harder. "I'll keep that in mind," she said between gritted teeth, then lay back down on the floor.

"Don't you think Eddie's cute?" Jenny went on.

Jessica looked at her with despair. "Of course I think he's cute. Jen, I'm really trying to concentrate, OK?"

Jenny began to giggle. "You'll never believe what he told me tonight. He said that he still can't tell you and Elizabeth apart sometimes. He said that a few days ago he went running up to Liz and said something to her and was embarrassed when he found out it was her and not you."

Jessica stared at her cousin, her exercises forgotten. "Eddie said *that*?" she repeated incredulously.

Jenny nodded. "Isn't that sweet? He's the most adorable boy in the world, Jess."

"Adorable," Jessica muttered. She wished she could find the idea as appealing as Jenny apparently did.

Jessica was used to people confusing her with Elizabeth; it happened all the time. But she wouldn't have guessed Eddie would make that mistake at this point!

Jessica jumped to her feet and crossed the crowded room to her dresser. The same old Jessica Wakefield stared back from her mirror, the same soft blond hair, the same aquamarine eyes.

"Well, he'll just have to get to know me a little better," Jessica said defiantly, more to herself than to Jenny. She was thinking that by the time she was through with Eddie Winters, he wouldn't make that mistake again!

Six

"Hey, Liz!" Jeffrey French called, hurrying to catch up with Elizabeth as she crossed the emerald lawn of Sweet Valley High toward the shade of a large tree.

Elizabeth felt her cheeks burn as she remembered what Jenny had told her about Jeffrey and Lila. Irrational as it seemed, she didn't want to talk to Jeffrey. Why had he bothered to give her the impression he'd try to go to the game the night before if he had intended to go dancing with Lila and Jessica all along?

"I was hoping I could convince you to have lunch with me," Jeffrey said, slightly out of breath from jogging.

Elizabeth looked briefly up into his friendly green eyes and glanced away again. "I've got some reading to do," she said coolly, sitting down on the soft grass under the tree.

Jeffrey crouched down beside her. "You sound mad," he observed. There was a tone of concern in his voice. "Have I done something to bug you?"

Elizabeth blinked. She wasn't used to guys who were as forthright as Jeffrey. She had just assumed he'd go away.

"I'm not mad," she said simply, avoiding his penetrating gaze.

"Come on," Jeffrey said lightly. He put his hand on her arm, and Elizabeth reddened. His hand was so warm!

"Well, I have to admit I was kind of surprised when my cousin told me she'd spent the evening with you at the Beach Disco," Elizabeth said finally. "I thought you were planning on going to the volleyball game to meet Enid."

"And I thought *you* were going to be with your cousin," Jeffrey said.

Elizabeth swallowed. "But I—"

"You said you couldn't go to the game because you had promised to do something with Jenny," Jeffrey cut in. "So it seems to me that if anyone around here has a right to be mad—"

Elizabeth stared at him, completely confused. "Well—I mean, I guess . . ."

Jeffrey shook his head. "You Wakefield twins," he said with mock severity. "Don't you think things are confusing enough for a guy as it is?"

Elizabeth gulped. Something in the tone of Jeffrey's voice. . . . It wasn't possible that he'd gone to the disco just because she'd said she was going to be with Jenny, was it?

"Did Lila ask you to go to the Beach Disco last night?" she blurted out at last.

Jeffrey smiled. "Yes. She and Jessica said they were taking Jenny there. They wanted to show her around. I just assumed if Jenny was going, you'd be going, too."

Elizabeth felt distinctly uncomfortable. Unless she was reading the situation wrong, it sounded as though Jeffrey were trying to hint that he'd made his mind up because of *her*.

She couldn't believe a mix-up like this could have happened! Jeffrey wasn't supposed to be interested in her. He was supposed to be interested in Enid!

And what kind of best friend, she wondered, would promise to fix her friend up with a fabulous new guy—and then steal him for herself?

*   *   *

"Liz, I've got to think of some way to get Jeffrey to notice me," Enid moaned. The girls were standing by Elizabeth's locker, watching the traffic swirl past them as the last-period bell sounded. "Are you going to see him this afternoon at the *Oracle* office?" Enid asked hopefully.

Elizabeth swallowed. "Probably," she said unenthusiastically. She was beginning to wish she had never gotten involved in any of this. The prospect of seeing Jeffrey again made her feel distinctly uneasy. Not that she didn't like him, because she did. She liked him a lot.

"I don't know, Enid," she said, trying to make her voice sound natural. "Maybe you should try to get to know Jeffrey on your own. I don't think I'm doing very well as a matchmaker."

Enid's green eyes filled with hopelessness. "Liz, don't abandon me!" she begged. "Honestly, if Lila campaigns any harder, she'll get him for sure! I need your help, Liz. I'm serious!"

Elizabeth's face darkened. "Why, what's Lila up to now? Has she given him a new camera yet?"

Enid shook her head and sighed. "Worse. I heard from Olivia that Lila's given him a new camera *and* a new tripod. Only Jeffrey wouldn't accept either of them. He said they were way too expensive!"

Elizabeth grinned. "At least he's ethical," she pointed out. "That means he may not let Lila buy him, much as she'd like to!"

"Buy him . . ." Enid repeated, a strange expression crossing her face. The next minute she snapped her fingers. "Liz, I've got it!"

"Got what?" Elizabeth asked uneasily, putting her books into her locker and taking out her knapsack.

"I just came up with the most wonderful plan," Enid said enthusiastically. "Liz, all you have to do is convince Jeffrey to sell himself at the auction on Friday. Then *I* can buy him!"

"Sell himself?" Elizabeth repeated, perplexed. "What do you mean?"

Enid's green eyes sparkled. "You know, sell a date with himself. I'll make sure to bid higher than anyone else does, and I'll finally get a chance to get to know him better!"

"How are you going to bid higher than Lila?"

Enid frowned. "We'll just have to come up with some way to make sure Lila doesn't show up at the auction. Come on, Liz, don't you think it's a great plan?"

"Well," Elizabeth said, thinking fast, "it's novel, I'll grant you that. Only what makes you think Jeffrey will consent to it? He seems to have such strong opinions about everything. I'm not sure he'll approve of 'selling' a date!"

Enid thought this over. "True," she conceded. "I know!" she exclaimed a few moments later. "Tell him it's a custom for new students, a kind of long-standing Sweet Valley High joke. And just remind him it's for charity and everything."

Elizabeth laughed. "I have to admit, you have it all worked out. I'll tell you what. I'll ask him and see what he says. But *you* have to think of some way to keep Jessica and Lila from showing up at the auction!"

"You've got a deal!" Enid exclaimed. "You'd better call me the minute you get home and let me know what he says, OK?"

"OK," Elizabeth said, smiling. She wanted to do everything she could to help her friend, but she couldn't help worrying that Jeffrey would take her suggestion the wrong way. What was going to keep him from guessing she was hoping to make the highest bid for him herself?

"Hey, those shots are wonderful," Elizabeth said, looking at a contact sheet over Jeffrey's shoulder. The *Oracle* office was deserted; she and

Jeffrey were the last ones there for the second time that week.

"You really think so?" Jeffrey asked, looking up at her, his eyes intent. "I've been afraid to show you any of my pictures."

"Why?" Elizabeth asked, surprised. "You're an excellent photographer, Jeffrey. You shouldn't be insecure!"

"I'm usually not, but I really care about what you think," he said simply.

Elizabeth took a deep breath. "You should show some of these to Enid," she said casually. "She knows a lot more about photography than I do."

Jeffrey looked quizzically at her but didn't respond. Once again Elizabeth had the strange sensation that she was doing something wrong.

"Uh—Jeffrey," she said, hastily backing away toward her own desk, "I was just wondering about the auction on Friday. I mentioned to you yesterday, when we were talking, that I was doing a story on it."

Jeffrey nodded. "Need any help?"

Elizabeth thought fast. "As a matter of fact, I do. It's going to sound kind of strange, but how would you like to offer your services—for a very good cause?"

"I'd love to," Jeffrey said, smiling at her.

75

"Honestly, Liz, any time you need help, just say the word."

"The thing is," Elizabeth said quickly, her cheeks burning, "we need a few more things to auction off. Winston Egbert is the auctioneer, and he mentioned it to me this morning."

"Maybe my mother has some things lying around the house," Jeffrey suggested.

Elizabeth shook her head. "This isn't really that kind of auction. Usually people sell really silly things: Last year Penny auctioned off a back rub, and Ken Matthews auctioned off the football he used to make the winning pass in the last game of the season. It's always that sort of thing."

"I'm not sure what *I* could auction," Jeffrey said thoughtfully. "Do you have any ideas?"

"Well," Elizabeth said, "why not auction off a date with yourself?"

Jeffrey blushed. "That won't bring in a whole lot of bids," he protested.

Elizabeth felt more uncomfortable than ever. "I'm sure a lot of people would give their right arm for an evening with you," she mumbled. *I can think of at least two*, she added to herself.

Jeffrey looked at her. "You really think that'll work?" he asked. "Won't it seem really— egotistical?"

"Oh, not at all," Elizabeth assured him. "Everyone chips in at the auction, and the whole mood is really silly. No one will think you usually get your dates this way," she added, her turquoise eyes twinkling.

"Well," Jeffrey said, "if you really think it's a good idea . . ."

"Oh, I do," Elizabeth said firmly. "I'm sure it'll be the best part of the whole auction!"

"I doubt that," Jeffrey said dryly. He turned back to his photographs. "If *you* win, Liz, we could finally take that tour of Sweet Valley," he added lightly.

Elizabeth swallowed. She was sure Jeffrey thought she had just set the whole plan up so she could ask him out.

And for some reason, it bothered her that he should think that. More than it ought to!

Elizabeth and Jeffrey were in the parking lot together half an hour later, saying goodbye to each other before heading to their cars to drive home.

"Jeffrey!" a high, feminine voice called. It was Lila Fowler sticking her head out of her lime-green Triumph. She had slowed her car down almost to a standstill, and, catching sight of Jeffrey, slid her stick shift into park.

"Hi, Lila," Jeffrey said conversationally.

"I'm so glad I caught you. I got tickets to that game I was telling you about," Lila said excitedly.

"You mean the pro soccer game in Los Angeles? But that's tonight!" Jeffrey said.

"I know. If we're going to be on time, we've got to get going!" Lila cried. "Why don't you leave your car here? I've got some sandwiches. We can head to L.A. right now!"

"Lila, I don't know if I can—"

"Jeffrey," Lila pouted, "if you had any idea how much trouble I went through to get these tickets, you wouldn't be giving me such a hard time!"

"Well," Jeffrey said, giving Elizabeth a searching look, "if you really went through so much trouble . . ."

A few minutes later the whole thing had been arranged, and Jeffrey hopped into the passenger's seat, looking as if he didn't know what had hit him.

Elizabeth walked slowly toward the Fiat. She knew it wasn't any of her business what Lila or Jeffrey did. Besides, she was beginning to realize Jeffrey wasn't that interested in getting to know

Enid. So why did she feel as though she could kill Lila right then? Unless . . .

But Elizabeth didn't want to think about the reason why she was so upset. She didn't want to think about anything at all.

Life just seemed too complicated all of a sudden. And it seemed the less she thought about things the better!

Seven

Friday morning Elizabeth was up especially early. She had a lot to do before the auction, which was going to be held in the auditorium that afternoon. She sat at the breakfast table, shuffling through the papers in her auction file, trying to concentrate.

When Jenny came into the kitchen, Elizabeth was chewing on her pen, a distracted expression in her eyes.

"Liz, is anything wrong?" her cousin asked, pouring herself a glass of orange juice and joining her at the table.

Elizabeth looked at Jenny as if she had never

seen her before. "Uh—I'm sorry, Jen, did you say something to me?"

Jenny giggled. "You're acting so funny lately, Liz. You seem like you're lost in space!"

Elizabeth blushed. "I'm just feeling a little overworked," she said. "All this stuff for *The Oracle* has been getting to me, but everything should calm down after this week."

"You know," Jenny said conversationally, "according to the book I'm reading right now, there are three ways to tell when someone's in love."

"Really?" Elizabeth said absently. "What are those?"

Jenny smiled mysteriously. "Well, according to the doctor who wrote the book, the first sign is being totally absentminded about everything." Jenny waited for her cousin's reaction and then continued. "The next biggie is blushing. Supposedly falling in love makes you embarrassed all the time."

Elizabeth frowned. "It sounds to me like this doctor hasn't really come up with very earth-shaking news, Jen. What's the third thing?"

"Loss of appetite," Jenny said sagely, opening a box of doughnuts and helping herself to two. "Want one?" she asked, thrusting the box at Elizabeth.

"No, thanks," Elizabeth said, picking up her file and standing. She was thinking so hard about Jeffrey and Enid that she'd barely registered what her cousin had said. Nor did she have any idea why Jenny doubled over with laughter when she added, "I'm not hungry this morning."

Jessica's right, Elizabeth thought as she watched her cousin dissolve into giggles. *The girl gets stranger every year.*

God only knew how Jessica was going to survive taking her along on her date with Eddie that evening!

Jessica had just cornered Enid in the hallway, hoping to find out through some skillful questioning whether Enid and Elizabeth had finally dropped their campaign on Jeffrey, when Lila Fowler accosted them.

"Enid! Liz!" She came hurrying up to the girls in the hallway, her arms filled with books. "I *have* to talk to you two. Has either of you seen Jessica?"

"That isn't funny, Lila," Jessica said coldly, eyeing her friend with contempt. "I'm sick and tired of twin jokes, if you want to know the truth."

Lila clapped her hand over her mouth. "Jess!" she gasped. The next minute she began to laugh. "You know, I honestly thought you were Liz," she said apologetically. "I guess it was because you were standing with Enid. And isn't that Elizabeth's sweater?" she added critically, frowning at Jessica's outfit.

Jessica's voice rose angrily. "It's *my* sweater, believe it or not. For goodness' sake, you'd think for once in my life I could have something that's mine and mine alone!"

"Good heavens," Lila said, looking at Enid with lifted eyebrows. "Aren't we touchy today?"

Enid grinned. "You're not having an identity crisis, are you, Jess?"

Jessica's eyes flashed. "No," she said shortly. "I'm having every other kind of crisis, though. Can you imagine spending your first real date with the man of your dreams taking care of the brattiest little cousin on earth?"

"No wonder you're in such a foul mood," Lila said sympathetically. "Privacy is *so* important when you're just getting to know a guy. Take Jeffrey and me," she ventured.

Enid flinched. She had no idea whether or not Lila knew that she liked Jeffrey, too. There was no telling whether Lila's remark was accidental or intentional.

"We had such a wonderful time the other night in L.A.," Lila continued. For the next few minutes, she held forth on what a perfect evening it had been. Enid held her breath, fighting for self-control. *Just wait*, she told herself. She was going to be sure to bid highest for Jeffrey at the auction that afternoon, and that would entitle her to an evening alone with him that very night! Lila would die if she knew.

"Hey, Enid," Jessica said suddenly, as if she'd been reading her mind, "you're in charge of the committee for the auction this afternoon, right?"

"Yep," Enid said casually. "Why, Jess? Are you interested in helping out?"

"Helping out?" Jessica repeated. "What do you mean?"

"Well, as a matter of fact, I was about to ask you before Lila came up. But, Lila, you should be in on this, too. The committee needs two volunteers to help pack up cans of food to take over to city hall when we're done with the auction. If you two are coming to the auction, we could really use your help."

"Packing cans of food?" Lila said distastefully. "You mean, actually putting them in boxes?"

"That's right," Enid said with a smile. "We'd need you to start at two, when the auction begins, and work through until five. How does that sound to you?"

Jessica and Lila exchanged glances. "Well, to tell you the truth, Enid," Jessica said quickly, "I promised Robin I'd go over some special routines for the cheerleaders this afternoon. Since we don't have classes because of the auction, we thought that would give us some extra time to iron out some of our moves."

"What about you, Lila?" Enid said with feigned hopefulness.

Lila flinched. "Well, I'd really love to help out, Enid. It sounds like such a worthwhile cause and everything. But I just remembered I've got a—uh, a doctor's appointment this afternoon."

"You're sure?" Enid said.

Lila nodded solemnly. "I'm really sorry, though," she repeated, winking at Jessica.

"Well," Enid said, making a note on the piece of paper she had clipped to her clipboard, "I'll keep an eye out for both of you in case you change your minds. If you show up, I'll be sure to point you in the right direction so you can help out since you're both so interested!"

Enid smiled as she watched the two girls hurry away together. She was impressed with her own ingenuity. She couldn't imagine anything in the world that would convince either Jessica or Lila to come to the auction now!

"Step right up, ladies and gentlemen, step right up!" Winston Egbert boomed into the microphone. Elizabeth burst out laughing when she saw him. Winston had come up with a ludicrous costume for the occasion—an old tuxedo with tails and a shabby top hat. A red bandanna tied around his neck completed the look.

It was two o'clock, and the auditorium was thronged with students. All week students had been stockpiling canned food in the boxes set up in the auditorium, and that day's auction would bring in even more food for the needy. Everyone had brought as many cans of food from home as he or she could carry, and students were already eagerly scheming to put their cans together so they could make joint bids on things they really wanted. Elizabeth scanned the crowd for Enid, but her friend was nowhere in sight. Jessica wasn't around, either, nor was Lila. Elizabeth wondered if Enid was acting as decoy somewhere to keep them busy. She just hoped her friend showed up in time to bid for Jeffrey!

Suddenly Elizabeth spotted Enid, and a smile broke over her face. She couldn't believe it. Enid was staggering under a box filled with dozens of cans of food, many more than anyone else had!

"Help," Enid gasped, setting the box down beside Elizabeth. "I have another of these out in the car," she added, wiping her brow.

"Looks like you really mean business," Elizabeth said, laughing. "What happened to Lila and Jessica? Did you find some way to get them off the scent?"

Grinning, Enid relayed her ploy. "You have to admit that it was inspired!" she concluded. "Wild horses couldn't drag either of them to this auditorium this afternoon!"

Elizabeth shook her head admiringly. "You're amazing, Enid. I never would've guessed you had it in you!"

"Shh," Enid said. "It looks like they're getting started."

"Ladies, gentlemen, and assorted others!" Winston boomed into the microphone. "Welcome to the third annual auction for the food drive. I don't mind telling you folks that today's auction is *really* special. We have twenty-five—count them—twenty-five wonderful things to auction off this afternoon, so if you'll just keep your hats on, we can get started as soon as I review the rules."

Everyone listened intently as Winston

explained how to make a bid. "It has to be done by cans," he reminded them. "Forty cans was the biggest bid we had last year, that was for the prized football that Ken Matthews threw in that famous touchdown against Palisades. So remember—put your hand straight up and I'll call on you. State your bid in a loud, clear voice. Are we ready?"

"*Ready!*" the audience roared.

"OK. Now the first thing we're auctioning off today is"—Winston paused dramatically, holding an index card up to the light—"a pair of tickets to see The Number One in Reis Stadium a week from tonight!"

Everyone clapped wildly. Roger Patman bid six cans of food; Ken Matthews bid seven; Aaron Dallas bid eight; a sophomore girl bid ten; Ken went to twelve; and after thunderous applause, Roger bid fifteen.

"And the tickets go to Roger Barrett Patman for fifteen cans!" Winston hollered. The audience went wild.

Elizabeth listened with amusement as item after item was auctioned off. A tape recorded by The Droids, Sweet Valley High's very own rock group. A voucher for a homemade dinner cooked by none other than Mr. Collins. The red pencil Mr. Jaworski, the history teacher, used to mark exams. A candid snapshot of Bruce Patman, Roger's cousin, in a bathing suit. Each of these items was met with wild applause, and by the time Jeffrey French came onstage, the audience was incredibly rowdy.

"Last but not least," Winston intoned, "we have a very special item, ladies and gentlemen. How high will the bids go for tonight on the town with Sweet Valley High's newest eligible bachelor—Jeffrey French?"

Everyone started cheering, and Elizabeth caught her breath, wondering what Enid would do.

"Ten cans!" a pretty sophomore named Stacie Cabot shrieked from the front row.

"Fifteen cans!" Caroline Pearce, a redheaded girl in the junior class, chimed in.

"Twenty cans," Stacie said, looking annoyed.

"Twenty-five," Caroline said, pouting.

Enid put her hand up, and a hush fell over the auditorium. "Ladies and gentlemen, we have another bidder!" Winston declared. "Enid Rollins, what's your bid for a date this evening with the inimitable Jeffrey French?"

"Seventy-five cans," Enid said. The audience went wild.

"Ladies and gentlemen, I have to beg you to

be quiet," Winston said, obviously agitated. "Seventy-five cans?" he repeated incredulously.

Enid just nodded. Caroline and Stacie were crestfallen. The bidding was over, and Enid had won a date with Jeffrey French.

"You did it!" Elizabeth exclaimed, giving her friend a hug. She could see Jeffrey descending the stage steps, and she knew any minute he'd come over to make arrangements with Enid for that evening.

Enid had finally managed to arrange some time alone with Jeffrey. Elizabeth knew she ought to be happy for her friend. So then, why did she feel as though she was about to burst into tears?

Eight

"Well, what do you two feel like doing now?" Eddie asked as he, Jessica, and Jenny came out of the Plaza Theater, where they had just seen the three-hour, black-and-white film version of *Wuthering Heights*.

"That was the most wonderful movie I've ever seen," Jenny gushed. "Jess, didn't you think Heathcliff was the most romantic creature in the whole world?"

Jessica glared at her. She couldn't believe what a disaster the evening was turning out to be. As far as she was concerned, the movie they had just seen was an utter waste of time. It was the sort of thing Mr. Collins made them watch in English class.

"I don't know, Eddie," she said sweetly, turning to him and ignoring her cousin's remark. "Maybe someplace quiet where we can really *talk*." Anyone other than her cousin would have taken that remark as a hint, she thought furiously. But Jenny seemed oblivious.

"We could go to the Dairi Burger," she said hopefully, her eyes fixed on Eddie's. The Dairi Burger, a popular hamburger place, was almost always jammed with students from Sweet Valley High.

Jessica had to admit her cousin looked better than usual that night. Her short brown hair was brushed neatly, and she had left her thick glasses at home, wearing contact lenses, which she apparently reserved for special occasions. Her eyes were actually her best feature—large, brown, and almost always sparkling with excitement—though Jessica found the things that excited her cousin unbelievably weird.

But even the dark-colored dress Jenny was wearing did little to disguise the fact that she was chubby. If only the girl would stick to three meals a day! Jessica thought. Personally she had no desire for a hamburger, not after a big dinner and popcorn and soda at the movie. But Jenny seemed to have forgotten her resolve to watch her diet.

"I'm famished," she declared. "It must be the air out here in California or something, but I feel like I could eat a horse!"

Jessica glowered. She couldn't imagine Jenny eating like a bird back home in Dallas. "I don't really feel like food right now," she objected.

But Eddie and Jenny seemed to be on identical wavelengths. "I could really go for a burger myself right now," Eddie said enthusiastically. The next thing Jessica knew, the three of them were jammed in Eddie's tiny car, heading over to the Dairi Burger. Jessica was in the middle, sitting on the bump, and Jenny's elbow kept poking her in the side. Even worse, Jenny and Eddie were talking animatedly to each other across her.

"I just love romantic novels, don't you?" Jenny asked.

"Actually, I like mysteries better," Eddie said. A lively discussion followed, which Jessica couldn't follow. She felt hot, uncomfortable, and irritated. The worst thing was that her interest in Eddie was diminishing rapidly. Why did he have to be such a creep whenever Jenny was around? Any normal guy would recognize her for the nerd she was and just ignore her. Instead, *she* was the one who was being ignored. And it was driving her straight up a wall.

By the time they were seated in a corner booth at the Dairi Burger, things had gotten even worse. Jenny and Eddie were talking about music—*classical* music. Jessica just sat there in stony silence, sipping angrily at her diet Coke.

"I think I like Mozart better than Schubert," Jenny said animatedly. "He has much more *complexity*, don't you think?"

Jessica snorted. Eddie stared at her, and she quickly feigned a paroxysm of coughing. "I have something in my throat," she said apologetically.

But it didn't matter anyway. Eddie wouldn't have noticed even if she had collapsed right there on the table. He was so busy ranting about composers.

Jessica was trying to decide whether or not this was really the worst evening she had ever had when she saw something that almost made her choke in earnest. "Jenny, look!" she shrieked, grabbing her cousin's arm.

"Look at what?" Jenny demanded, her eyes following Jessica's stare.

"Jeffrey French," Jessica hissed, "is sitting over at that booth with *Enid Rollins*!"

"So?" Jenny said blandly, taking a big bite of her double cheeseburger.

Jessica glanced at her cousin with contempt. "Oh—never mind," she said acidly, jumping to her feet and hurrying across the crowded, noisy room.

Jenny didn't understand anything! How in the world had Enid managed to get Jeffrey to take her out? Jessica was aghast, and she knew Lila would kill her if she didn't find out as much as she possibly could.

"Enid! Jeff!" she called sweetly, pretending she had just noticed the couple as she swept past their booth. "What a *surprise*!"

Jeffrey smiled at Jessica. "Who are you here with, Jess? Do you want to join us for a few minutes?"

"I'd love to," Jessica declared, plopping down on the bench next to Enid so the girl had to slide down and was no longer opposite Jeffrey. "What brings you two here together this evening?" she asked, putting a slight emphasis on the word *together*. Enid turned crimson, and neither spoke.

"We're just having a couple of the best burgers in town, that's all," Jeffrey said, giving Enid a wink.

Jessica looked at him thoughtfully. He really was awfully good-looking. Was it possible he

97

was deranged enough to consider Enid Rollins entertaining?

"Jess, will you excuse me for a second?" Enid asked.

"Sure," Jessica said, bouncing up to let her get past. The minute Enid was out of earshot she leaned forward, her eyes bright with curiosity. "Jeff, are you and Enid going out?" she asked. She managed to make it sound like something approximately equal to catching the plague.

"We are tonight," Jeffrey said cheerfully. "Enid won my company at the auction this afternoon," he added. "And to tell you the truth, I feel pretty flattered. I was sure no one would bid for me at all!"

Jessica stared at him, her eyes enormous. "You mean"—she gasped—"you were part of the auction, and Lila and I. . . ." She gaped at him, the full truth dawning on her. Enid had made sure that she and Lila stayed away from the auction. Enid—and Elizabeth!

Jeffrey looked quizzically at her. "What's wrong? I didn't say something I shouldn't have, did I?"

"No," Jessica said furiously. "You didn't, Jeff. It isn't your fault." She was too angry to say anything more. That scheming, no-good twin of hers! Elizabeth had really tricked her. And even though Jessica adored her sister, right then she was enraged!

So that was why Enid had asked her and Lila to help pack cans after the auction. Enid had made sure that neither of them would go to the auction, leaving her and Elizabeth free to follow through on their little scheme.

And it had worked, too! That was the very worst part. Jessica never would have guessed her very own flesh and blood could have been involved in anything so low and deceitful.

"Jeff, I've got to go back to my table," she said quickly, getting to her feet. She barely heard what he said in reply. She was too busy fuming—and too busy trying to cook up a scheme that would seal the relationship between Jeffrey and Lila.

Jessica had been halfhearted about fixing Lila and Jeffrey up until that moment. But from then on her whole heart and soul were going to be involved.

Somehow or other, Jessica was going to find a way to get back at her twin and Enid. Whatever it took, she was going to get even!

"What should we do now?" Jeffrey asked.

They had left the Dairi Burger and were sitting in his car.

Enid chewed nervously on her lip. "I don't know," she said. "We could just sort of drive around . . . maybe go down to the beach."

"Fine," Jeffrey said, but he didn't start the car up. He was obviously thinking about something, and for the millionth time Enid wished she knew what he was thinking.

"I've got an idea," Jeffrey said at last, giving her a warm smile. "Why don't we head over to the Beach Disco and see if anyone from school is there?"

Enid took a deep breath. "OK," she said at last. She had been hoping for something a little more romantic, but the truth was, Jeffrey didn't seem very interested in romance. Not with her, anyway.

It wasn't that he hadn't been a wonderful date. He had come inside when he picked her up and made Enid's mother relax with his natural sense of humor and easygoing style. He was being a perfect gentleman, opening the door on Enid's side of the car, holding her jacket for her when she slipped into it, listening attentively to everything she said.

But she could tell Jeffrey wasn't interested. In the first place, he had suggested they drop by the Dairi Burger for something to eat. The Dairi Burger was fun, but it wasn't exactly a romantic spot! Bright lights and jukebox music, that was what the Dairi Burger had to offer. Even the topics of conversation Jeffrey kept broaching were strictly casual. He asked her questions about school, steering their talk toward light, impersonal matters. He talked a little bit about himself, but, again, he kept it very light, mentioning his love of soccer and his commitment to photography. In fact, more than once Enid had the distinct impression he was trying to let her know how busy he was, as though he were letting her down lightly.

But Enid didn't feel so disappointed. Jeffrey was very nice, but she could see they weren't that well-suited. She was actually relieved. Going out with him had all turned into a big deal, and she had been feeling more than a little uneasy about the whole thing. She secretly believed things either clicked right from the start or they never would. And obviously things with Jeffrey and her just weren't clicking!

The rest of the evening passed very quickly. Jeffrey seemed to relax once they were lost in the crowd at the disco, and they actually had fun dancing together. Enid found herself wondering if she had been wrong.

But when Jeffrey dropped her off an hour or two later, she knew her instincts had been right.

"I had a nice time tonight," he said, patting her hand with a fond smile. "Thanks for spending all those cans on me!"

Enid laughed. "Oh, you can always count on me," she said stupidly. Then the two of them just stared at each other. "Well . . . good night," Enid said lamely.

Jeffrey looked every bit as awkward and embarrassed as she felt! Enid couldn't wait to get out of the car and into the house. She wanted nothing more than to race up to her bedroom, slam the door closed, and call Elizabeth.

Anything this embarrassing was too painful to keep to herself. Thank heavens she had a best friend to share it with!

Nine

"How do I look, Jess?" Jenny asked, twirling around in a navy blue bathing suit.

Jessica resisted the temptation to tell her the truth. "You look fine," she said testily, digging through the pile of clothing on her bed in search of one of her bikinis. It was Sunday morning, and ordinarily Jessica would still be sound asleep. But Jenny had been up for hours, playing classical music on the stereo and making all sorts of crashing and banging noises. A person would have to be deaf to stay in bed with Jennifer Townsend around.

But for once Jessica didn't mind being up early. She had plenty of things to organize before the big beach party that afternoon, which had been organized as the final event of the PTA Food-Drive Week. Apart from everything else, she had been hoping to sit out by the pool in the backyard for an hour or two. She was convinced her tan had faded, and if there was anything Jessica hated, it was showing up at the beach looking like a ghost.

Jessica's plan to get revenge on Elizabeth and Enid had taken shape the day before on the phone with Lila. The thing that bothered Jessica most was that Elizabeth had dared to scheme behind her back. That was so unlike her twin, and Jessica didn't want it to become a regular practice! No, this uncharacteristic plotting would have to be stopped immediately. Once Elizabeth realized she couldn't outfox Jessica, everything would be back to normal.

The main thing was that Jessica couldn't stomach the thought of Enid and Jeffrey as a couple. It wasn't that Enid wasn't nice. She was nice—nice and boring! As far as Jessica was concerned, Enid was a bad influence on her sister. Enid liked dull things and dull people. What kind of best friend was that?

Take Enid's attitude to the sorority, for example. Elizabeth and Jessica had pledged Pi Beta Alpha, the exclusive sorority at school, at the same time as Enid. But Jessica was the only one of the three to take it seriously. Now she was president, as devoted and hardworking a member as she could be. Enid and Elizabeth, however, treated it with total indifference, if not contempt. Elizabeth claimed she had only gone through pledge period for Jessica's sake, a sentiment Jessica was sure originated with Enid. Enid was always making trouble for her sister!

And now this. The last thing in the world Jessica could fathom was allowing Enid to drive a wedge between her twin sister and herself. Jessica was sure that on her own Elizabeth would never dream of fixing up Enid and Jeffrey French. It had to have been Enid's idea, and Jessica felt obligated to demonstrate how foolish an idea it had been.

She and Lila were ready for them. Whatever Enid and Elizabeth had planned, they wouldn't be able to outsmart Jessica and Lila. Lila had already called Jeffrey and convinced him to accept a ride to the beach with her that afternoon. Her plan was to do whatever it took to keep Jeffrey at her side all afternoon, thus ensuring that Jeffrey didn't so much as get a chance to see Enid. Now that Jessica had told Lila that Enid and Elizabeth were scheming against her, Lila was filled with resolve as well as fury.

And when Lila Fowler really wanted something, there was one thing you could count on—she would get it!

"This is great!" Jenny said appreciatively, looking around at the expanse of white sand. The party included a cookout, dancing, games, and prizes. The PTA had transformed the strip of beach, setting up gaily colored tents, volleyball nets, and a temporary wooden dance floor near the bandstand. The Droids were warming up on a small raised dais near the dance floor. Everything looked terrific, and the smells of barbecued hot dogs mixed with the salty tang of the ocean were delightful!

But Elizabeth was in no mood to appreciate the festive atmosphere of the party. Everything had gone wrong so far that day, absolutely everything. She and Enid had planned to get there early, but Jessica had slipped out and taken the Fiat, without even leaving a note of explanation. She had also left Jenny. And both Mr. and Mrs. Wakefield had taken their cars to run errands. Despairing, Elizabeth had called Enid to see if she could borrow her mother's car, but Mrs.

Rollins had gone out for the day, too. In the end, Elizabeth, Enid, and Jenny had been forced to take the bus, which seemed to take ages to show up. Instead of being the first to arrive, they were almost the last. The party was in full swing, with students milling around everywhere.

It took Elizabeth several minutes to locate Jeffrey in the crowd. "There he is," Elizabeth said urgently to Enid. "Now, remember. The plan is, I'll tell Jeffrey that we need some pictures for *The Oracle*, and I'll introduce him to a few of the PTA people, and then I'll tell him he needs to do a special photo series on the head of the student committee—namely, *you*."

"Liz, I don't know about this," Enid said weakly. "I told you, he really doesn't seem interested in me! Why force it?"

"Because," Elizabeth said fiercely, "you just can't give up. That's all there is to it!"

"But—"

"Enid," Elizabeth burst out in exasperation, "come on! You can't give up because he didn't bring you dozens of roses on the first date! Maybe he's just shy!"

"He isn't shy," Enid protested. "He just isn't interested in me."

"Nonsense," Elizabeth declared. "Honestly,

Enid! You can't be so negative about every-thing!"

Enid bit her lip. She couldn't understand why Elizabeth was so big on the idea of getting her together with Jeffrey, especially now, when it was so evident that no sparks had flown Friday evening.

Enid had done her very best to explain that she didn't care about things not working out with Jeffrey, but Elizabeth seemed oblivious to every-thing she said. For some reason Elizabeth insisted on getting the two together. The more Enid protested, the more determined Elizabeth became.

"Stay right here," Elizabeth said, her brow clearing as she spotted Jeffrey leading Lila toward the dance floor. "I'm going to grab him now—before Lila monopolizes him for the rest of the day!"

Enid watched her best friend charge away. She had no idea why Elizabeth was trying so hard, but she was certain of one thing: However hard Elizabeth pushed it, it just wasn't written in the stars for Jeffrey and Enid to fall in love!

"Jeffrey!" Elizabeth exclaimed.

Jeffrey glanced down from the dance floor.

"Liz!" he said. "I looked for you earlier, but I couldn't find you anywhere."

"Jeffie," Lila said with a pout, "this is my favorite song!"

"Let me just say hello to Liz for a second," Jeffrey said, strolling over to the edge of the dance floor toward the spot where Elizabeth was standing on the sandy beach. "How're you doing, stranger?" he asked, giving her a special smile.

Elizabeth's heart beat faster. "Uh—fine," she mumbled, averting her eyes. For a minute she forgot what she was doing over there, but one glance at Lila's irate face, and she remembered. Elizabeth couldn't believe the way Lila was acting. First of all, she was dressed inappropriately for a picnic on the beach. Her one-piece, white jumpsuit would have been more suitable on a Hollywood set. And those gold-spangled high heels were just too much. Elizabeth couldn't help thinking her outfit was way too lowcut, as well. She would have exposed the same amount of skin if she were wearing a bathing suit!

"Jeff, I hate to drag you away from the dance floor, but I really could use some help covering the party for *The Oracle*," Elizabeth said, shading her eyes with one hand as she squinted up at him in the bright sunlight.

Jeffrey looked at Lila, who had followed him to the edge of the dance floor. "Lila, if you'll just excuse me—"

"You *can't* spend the whole day running around with Liz and that dumb camera!" Lila exploded. Several students nearby turned to stare, but Lila didn't care. "Please, Jeffie," she said, "you promised we'd spend some time alone together today."

"Well, I feel bad about it," Jeffrey said sympathetically, "but I really owe it to the paper. I'm sure it won't take too long."

Lila was furious. "I'm sure it'll take forever," she said grumpily.

Elizabeth gave Jeffrey her most persuasive smile. "Come on, Jeff, let's go talk to Mr. Walters, the chairman of the food drive."

"I'm coming," Jeffrey said. Elizabeth couldn't help feeling triumphant as they walked off together, leaving Lila fuming behind them.

For the next twenty minutes Elizabeth and Jeffrey made the rounds from one PTA member to the next. Elizabeth did quick interviews, while Jeffrey snapped pictures. "That's wonderful," she said when they had finished the last profile.

"Can we take a breather?" Jeffrey asked, smiling at her. "I'd love to go for a swim with you. I bet you're wonderful in the water."

Elizabeth blushed. "Well, there's only one more person we still have to talk to," she told him.

"OK, boss," Jeffrey said, laughing. They walked along the beach together in silence for a minute. "Liz—" Jeffrey began.

"I'm going to leave you alone to do this piece, OK?" Elizabeth interrupted. "If you could just ask a few questions—you know, put together a very brief story to go with the pictures—"

Jeffrey eyed her thoughtfully. "OK," he said at last. "But I'd really rather do the story with you. Can I at least find you later on?"

Elizabeth's heart began to pound. She couldn't believe how confused she felt! "I guess so," she whispered, not meeting his gaze. "Oh, look!" she added quickly. "There's Enid!"

"Enid?" Jeffrey repeated blankly as they neared Elizabeth's friend, who was sitting on a deck chair, watching them with obvious embarrassment.

"Yes, Enid," Elizabeth said. "She's the one you have to interview. After all, she was in charge of the auction."

Jeffrey stared at Elizabeth, the blank expression on his face beginning to give way to one of mingled annoyance and embarrassment.

"I'll just leave you two alone," Elizabeth said

hastily. "Let me know if you have any questions, Jeff. I'll be talking to Mr. Collins about the story we're putting together."

"Elizabeth Wakefield!" Jessica hollered. "Wait right there. I've got to talk to you!"

An inquisitive smile on her face, Elizabeth turned to see her sister. They were safely out of earshot of Enid and Jeffrey, but Jessica's voice was gaining volume with every second. "How dare you," Jessica panted as she raced up to her twin. "Lila told me what you did just now. You dragged Jeffrey away from her just so you could get him together with Enid. I think it's disgusting."

Elizabeth's cheeks burned. "Well, it's no worse than you trying to fix him up with Lila, is it?"

Jessica glared at her. "Of all the sneaky, low-down tricks to play on your own sister! You two kept Lila and me from coming to the auction so Enid could win Jeffrey as her date," she added accusingly.

Elizabeth felt her own temper flaring. "So what?" she cried. "You and Lila kept Enid and me from coming to the pool party you had last week, didn't you?"

"Enid's all wrong for Jeffrey," Jessica retorted.

"Can't you see that, Liz? He doesn't care about her at all!"

Elizabeth felt tears start to well in her eyes. "Well, he doesn't seem to care very much about Lila, either," she snapped. "Jess, just leave me alone, OK?"

Jessica glared at her. "Suit yourself," she said angrily. The next minute she had stormed off down the beach, leaving Elizabeth alone.

Boy, Elizabeth thought, rubbing her temples. Life sure was getting complicated since Jeffrey got to town.

Several minutes later she was back at the spot where she had left Jeffrey and Enid. But something was wrong. Jeffrey had vanished!

"Where is he?" she asked Enid. She couldn't keep a note of accusation from creeping into her voice. "Did you let him get away?"

Enid looked up at Elizabeth, her green eyes filled with tears. "Liz, stop," she said. "Honestly, I appreciate what you're trying to do, but it just won't work! Can't you see that you're just making everything worse?"

Elizabeth stared at her friend in consternation. "You just have to try harder," she protested.

Enid shook her head desperately. "We really just don't make a good couple," she said truthfully. "Liz, I'd be the first to tell you if I were upset about it. I just want to forget the whole thing."

"But you *are* upset," Elizabeth pointed out. "You've been crying!"

"That's only because you've been torturing me," Enid said, smiling as she wiped a tear from her face. "If you just leave me alone, I'll be fine!"

Elizabeth shook her head. "Look, let me just go try to find Jeff. Give it one more chance," she pleaded. "Just for me, Enid!"

Enid's voice trembled. "Liz—"

But Elizabeth didn't hear her. She was already bounding off down the beach, looking for Jeffrey. It seemed to Elizabeth as if this were the very last chance to get Jeffrey and Enid together, and she felt as if she had to make one last desperate bid on her best friend's behalf.

Ten

"Jeffrey!" Elizabeth called. She could see the blond boy walking a couple of hundred yards from the farthest tent, his hair tousled from the breeze coming off the sea. The wind must have been too strong for him to hear her, Elizabeth thought, because he didn't turn around. Taking a deep breath, she began to jog after him. In a few minutes she had halved the distance between them, and she called his name again. This time he turned around.

"Hi," he said when she had caught up to him. For the first time, his green eyes were moody, and his expression looked almost sullen. "I thought you had things to do. I thought you had to talk to Mr. Collins," he said flatly.

Elizabeth blinked. "I—well, I did," she said hastily. "But then, when I went back to see how you and Enid were getting along, you weren't there. So I thought—"

"Listen, Liz," Jeffrey said, stopping in his tracks and facing her. "What's this business about Enid, anyway? Are you trying to play some kind of game with me?"

Elizabeth stared at him, her heart pounding. "What do you mean?" she whispered.

Jeffrey shrugged his shoulders helplessly. "I just can't figure it out. Every time I see you you're going on and on about how wonderful Enid is. Enid's so good at photography. Enid's the perfect one to give you a tour of Sweet Valley. And then today . . ." His voice trailed off uncertainly.

"Don't you think she's nice?" Elizabeth asked.

"Sure she's nice! What does that have to do with anything?"

Elizabeth was confused. "You just haven't really gotten to know her yet," she told him, trying another tack. "If you give her a chance—"

"Look," Jeffrey snapped, "I'm a big boy, Liz. I'm almost seventeen. I don't need any help choosing who I go out with."

Elizabeth felt the color drain from her face. "I was only trying to help," she said defensively. "Enid really cares about you, Jeffrey. It seems like the very least you could do is—"

"Stop it!" Jeffrey yelled, covering his ears with his hands. His eyes were fiery with anger now. "Listen to me," he said, putting his hands on her shoulders and giving her a little shake that was almost rough. "I think Enid Rollins is a nice girl, but that's it. *Period*. And if you don't mind, I think I can take care of my romantic life on my own!"

Elizabeth's eyes filled with tears. But before she had a chance to respond, Jeffrey had spun on his heels and stomped off, back in the direction of the party.

Then the tears came in earnest. Elizabeth sank down in the sand, watching the waves crash toward her, and tried to make some sort of sense out of the scene that had just occurred. It seemed she had really made a mess of everything. Jessica was furious with her for interfering and scheming behind her back. Enid was angry with her for becoming so insistent about Jeffrey. And Jeffrey . . .

Elizabeth put her face in her hands, her shoulders heaving. She couldn't believe the way Jeffrey had spoken to her just then. He had sounded so angry, as if he couldn't even stand talking to her! How could she have been such an idiot? Of course Jeffrey was old enough to choose his own girlfriends! And Enid hadn't even really wanted to keep trying, once she had a date with him and realized they weren't suited for each other.

No, it had all been her own fault. If she hadn't pushed so hard . . .

"Hey," a soft voice said, "is this a private sob session, or can I join you?"

Elizabeth lifted her tearstained face as Jessica's hand patted her shoulder reassuringly. "Oh, Jess," she said, weeping even harder at the sight of her twin's sympathetic face, "I've made such a mess of everything!"

Jessica crouched down in the sand next to her sister. "Don't be so hard on yourself," she said.

Elizabeth wiped the tears from her face. "Enid's furious with me," she said brokenly. "And you're mad at me . . ."

"Well," Jessica said judiciously, "I've thought the whole thing over, and I decided I was at least as wrong as you were."

Elizabeth's face brightened momentarily. "You mean you're not mad?" she said hopefully.

"Nope. As long as you don't make a habit out of this kind of thing," Jessica said generously.

Elizabeth's eyes darkened. "But Enid . . ."

"Why's Enid mad?" Jessica demanded. "It seems to me that you were doing her a real favor."

"Well, I guess I just didn't know when to stop. I kept pushing Jeffrey at her long after she'd lost interest."

"She'll forgive you," Jessica assured her. "Come on, Liz. It's not exactly the end of the world, is it?"

"But what about Jeffrey?" Elizabeth asked. "You should have heard the way he yelled at me a few minutes ago, Jess!"

"Jeffrey," Jessica said thoughtfully, "is not worth worrying about. To tell you the truth, I can't believe we've all been chasing him. He's completely average if you ask me."

Elizabeth's eyes widened. "He's not *average*," she objected.

"What's he really got going for him, anyway?" Jessica demanded, eyeing her sister closely.

Elizabeth thought quickly. "Well, he's—I don't know. . . . He's thoughtful, he's funny, he's interesting—"

"I guess I just don't see it," Jessica said.

"He's incredibly intelligent," Elizabeth went on defensively, obviously warming to her argument. "He's great-looking, too, in case you didn't notice. And he's really sensitive. That's why I feel like such a jerk for being so completely *in*sensitive all week, haranguing him about Enid."

"Liz," Jessica said, dragging her finger absently through the sand, "it sounds to me as though you kind of like Jeffrey. Am I right?"

"Like him?" Elizabeth repeated dumbly, her eyes round. "Do you mean—"

Jessica laughed. "For God's sake, Liz. You know what I mean! You sound as if you're completely, madly in love with this guy. You should hear yourself."

Elizabeth was astonished. "I do?"

"Yes," Jessica said, jumping to her feet. "You do!"

Elizabeth swallowed. Was it possible she had been falling in love with Jeffrey without even realizing it? That she had been pushing Enid toward him out of guilt, afraid that she would be cheating her friend by following her own heart?

"I feel like such a fool," she whispered, putting her chin in her hands. "Jess, I've acted like such an *idiot*."

"Well, none of us has been exactly acting like a brainchild this week." Jessica sighed. "Do you want to hear something that'll take your mind off your worries?"

120

"I sure do!" Elizabeth exclaimed.

"You're never going to believe this," Jessica said gloomily. "But guess who Eddie Winters is slow-dancing with at this very moment?"

Elizabeth stared at her twin. "Not—"

"Jenny," Jessica said sorrowfully. "Our nerdy little cousin. Apparently they're just *made* for each other. They love the same dumb books, the same dumb movies. . . ."

Elizabeth tried to suppress a giggle. "Poor Jess," she said sympathetically. "Are you really angry with her?"

Jessica shrugged philosophically. "I figure if Eddie is nuts about Jenny, he can't be worth bothering about. Come on, Liz. Let's go back to the party. We're wasting a wonderful afternoon!"

Elizabeth shook her head as she got to her feet. "I wish I could be as nonchalant about Jeffrey," she said sadly. "I don't know how I could have been so *stupid*!"

"You know," Jessica said, giving her sister a sly smile, "it's not exactly too late for you to tell Jeffrey you're sorry. You can't expect *everyone* to be as generous as I've been and make the first move!"

Elizabeth swallowed. She couldn't imagine

facing Jeffrey again. It all seemed too embarrassing.

Besides, she could barely work out how she felt about him. How would she be able to look him in the eye before she had faced up to her own innermost feelings?

"Jess! Liz!" Jenny came hurrying over to the twins with an enormous smile on her face. "I'm having such a good time today," she said excitedly, giving Jessica a big hug. "I can't believe it! And I owe it all to you, Jess. Eddie is the sweetest guy in the whole world."

"Yeah," Jessica said dryly, rolling her eyes at Elizabeth. *"Isn't* he."

"He's already trying to figure out some way to come visit me in Dallas," Jenny said dreamily. "Are you two hungry? I'm just dying for another hot dog."

The twins exchanged amused glances as Jenny heaped a paper plate full of food. "I thought you said love made people lose their appetites," Elizabeth said suddenly, remembering the conversation she and her cousin had had at breakfast earlier that week.

"Oh, Eddie and I aren't in love," Jenny said disdainfully, taking a big bite of a hot dog. "Are you kidding? We're just really good friends. Love is too stupid," she added, licking a bit of mustard off her hand.

Elizabeth laughed. "That's for sure," she said. Her stomach turned over as she caught sight of Jeffrey, moving toward the dance floor with Lila.

If only things were as simple for her as they were for her little cousin, she mused. She wished the feelings she had for Jeffrey were straightforward and uncomplicated. But they weren't.

Up until that very minute she really hadn't admitted the force of her emotions. But there was no denying it any longer: she was falling in love.

"Hey," Jenny said, giving her a nudge. "You've got that funny look on your face again, Liz. Is everything OK?"

Jessica laughed. "You're pretty perceptive, Jen, for someone who thinks love is stupid."

Jenny's eyes widened. "Liz, are you in love?" she whispered.

Elizabeth laughed hollowly. "Even if I were," she declared, "it wouldn't make any difference. I've made a real mess of things, I'm afraid. And I think this time it's just too late to work it out."

Jenny was fascinated. "Who is he?"

Elizabeth shook her head. "Let's just say he's the world's most wonderful guy," she said sorrowfully. "And your silly cousin has botched it up so badly that she's lost her chance to get to know him better!"

"The book I'm reading says it's never too late," Jenny said solemnly, popping the last bite of hot dog into her mouth.

Jessica burst out laughing. "Listen to her, Liz," she suggested. "She's the only one around here who seems to be getting anywhere!"

Elizabeth smiled, but her heart wasn't in it. She wished it weren't too late. But looking across the crowded beach to the dance floor, where Lila and Jeffrey were moving in each other's arms, she had a feeling Jenny was wrong.

It *was* too late. She had lost Jeffrey French forever.

Eleven

"Enid," Elizabeth said, putting her hand shyly on her friend's shoulder, "I want to talk to you for a minute."

Enid spun around, her eyes filling with tears when she saw her best friend's face. "You promise you're not going to try to convince me to give Jeffrey another chance?" she asked uncertainly.

The two girls walked away from the small crowd that had gathered at the main tent on the beach. "I promise," Elizabeth said sincerely. "Enid, I've acted like a real jerk. Will you just hear me out a few minutes before you judge me too harshly?"

"Of course!" Enid said. "Liz, after all you and I

have been through, I'm not going to let something this silly come between us!"

"Good," Elizabeth said, giving her a hug. "Thank heavens for that!"

"Tell me what's on your mind," Enid said as they sank down into beach chairs facing the ocean.

"Well, in the first place, my intentions were good right from the start!" Elizabeth said with a smile. "I knew you liked Jeffrey and I honestly wanted to help you get to know him. But I guess somewhere along the way I started to get to know him myself. And I think I got kind of mixed up about my own feelings."

Enid's eyes widened. "You mean *you're* interested in Jeffrey, too?" When Elizabeth nodded, Enid burst out laughing. "Jeffrey French sure has caused a lot of problems around here! He's only been in school a couple of weeks, and he's already got three girls fighting over him!"

Elizabeth reddened. "It's such a stupid situation," she admitted. "That's why I've decided just to back off and forget the whole thing. Besides, Lila looks like she really wants him. And I would never dare to compete with that!"

Enid's expression turned serious again. "How long have you been feeling this way?" she asked. "I don't understand, Liz. Why would you want to keep trying to get Jeffrey together with me if you cared about him yourself?"

"Good question." Elizabeth sighed. "I guess I didn't realize how I felt until this afternoon. Jessica was the one who confronted me. Oh, I've been such a dope, Enid! I mean, I kind of realized that I was feeling confused about everything, but I never really thought I, you know, *liked* him."

"Maybe that's why you kept trying so hard," Enid mused. "You're such a good friend, Liz. You probably felt guilty every time you suspected that you liked him, and instead of admitting it to yourself, you just increased your efforts on my behalf."

"Something like that," Elizabeth said ruefully. "Anyway, as long as you forgive me, then everything is OK again."

Enid was quiet for a minute. "Of course I forgive you," she said finally. "For one thing, there's really nothing to forgive. The important thing is that you know how you feel now."

Elizabeth didn't respond right away. "Well, as I said, I don't think it makes any difference. I'm not going to bother poor Jeffrey again."

Enid looked at her thoughtfully. "You and Jeffrey have spent a lot of time together this past week," she pointed out. "You probably know him as well as anyone else around here. Did you ever get the feeling that he cared for you?"

Elizabeth felt her cheeks getting hot. "Well—I don't know." She sighed. "I couldn't really tell. Maybe."

"Look," Enid said, "I hate to be the one to remind you of what you yourself said, but this isn't exactly the time to give up, is it? So you two had a couple of misunderstandings. Does that mean you should just forget the whole thing? I think you'd make a great couple," she added enthusiastically.

Elizabeth shook her head. "I'd never be able to look him in the face again," she said. "I feel stupid enough about the whole thing as it is."

"Oh, come on." Enid laughed. "You really need a dose of your own medicine! Who was it who was telling me that giving up is the worst thing to do?"

"But that was different," Elizabeth protested.

"I'm not going to let you off so easy," Enid vowed. "Liz, you have to talk to him. You have to tell him you're sorry. Even if you don't confess how you feel, you owe it to him to admit you've been trying to force me on him!"

Elizabeth stared at the sand. She knew Enid was right.

"All right," she said finally, reluctantly getting to her feet. "Here goes nothing!"

"Bravo!" Enid shrieked, clapping her hands in excitement. "I'll be crossing my fingers for you," she added, giving Elizabeth a pat on the back for encouragement.

Elizabeth's stomach took a dive as she walked across the beach toward the dance floor. She was glad Enid had her fingers crossed. Something told her she was going to need all the luck she could get!

"Excuse me," Elizabeth said, feeling more and more like a prize fool. "Can I cut in?"

Lila glared at her. "Jeffrey and I are *dancing*," she said icily. "Can't it wait?"

"Lila," Jeffrey said gently, "it's considered bad form if the reporter and the photographer don't dance at least one dance sometime this afternoon."

"Oh, all right," Lila said furiously, flouncing off across the dance floor. Elizabeth and Jeffrey exchanged glances, and the next minute both had begun to laugh.

"I'm sorry for intruding," Elizabeth said shyly.

A slow song was starting up, and Jeffrey took

her hand. "You have to relax," he said softly, "or we're never going to be able to dance."

The next minute she was in his arms, and the whole world made sense again. Elizabeth put her head against his shoulder. He smelled so clean, and his arms felt so warm around her. . . . She could feel her heart pounding as his arms held her close.

"You didn't come to find me so you could start that business up again about Enid, did you?" Jeffrey asked her.

Elizabeth's eyes swam with tears. "I'm so sorry," she said huskily. "I didn't mean to be so pushy, Jeffrey. Enid's my best friend, and I was just— I don't know. . . ." Her voice trailed off.

"Silly girl," Jeffrey said tenderly, resting his chin on her head as they danced. "Don't you realize I'm already taken?"

"Taken?" Elizabeth repeated stupidly. "You mean—"

"I mean I like Enid, but I couldn't be interested in her, because I'm in love with someone else."

"Oh," Elizabeth said, feeling as though the whole world had just crashed in on her. So he already had a girlfriend! So much for her stupid impression that he cared for *her*. She must have been out of her mind.

"Only she just doesn't seem to realize it,"

Jeffrey said softly, putting his hand under Elizabeth's chin and tilting it upward so he could look deep into her eyes.

Suddenly everything made sense. She only had to look at him to know what he meant. She didn't know what to say, but it didn't matter, for the next instant Jeffrey was leaning forward, and Elizabeth's eyes closed as his lips came closer. She had never felt a touch so gentle before in her whole life, and she just prayed that the kiss would last and last.

"I'm so glad you came up here and found me," Jeffrey whispered tenderly, tightening his arms around her.

Elizabeth smiled up at him, her eyes shining with tears. "Now that I've found you, I'm not going to let you go," she told him fiercely.

"Thank goodness for that!" Jeffrey said warmly. The Droids were beginning their newest song, "I Feel It for You," and Elizabeth felt as though she could have written the words herself.

What had started off as a terrible day was turning out to be a day that she would remember as the start of something unbelievably precious and wonderful. She had finally found a match for Jeffrey French. And something told her this one would last!

* * *

"Jess, I could kill you," Lila Fowler fumed. The beach party had ended, and Jessica was in the parking lot, loading things into the Fiat.

"What's the problem?" Jessica asked innocently.

"You know darned well what the problem is. That sister of yours has stolen Jeffrey right out of my arms!"

"He couldn't have been too happy there if he let himself be stolen," Jessica pointed out. "Come on, Lila. It could be a lot worse. He could have fallen for Jenny, like Eddie did."

Lila glared at her. "I am *livid*," she said furiously. "I don't think I'm ever going to be able to forgive either of you!"

Jessica smoothed the front of the new sundress she had slipped over her bikini. "You'll get over it," she said lightly. Jessica had weathered enough storms with Lila to know that this, too, would pass. "Anyway, I think Jeffrey and Liz make a cute couple. It's high time Liz met someone nice."

Lila looked horrified. "How can you *say* that? Isn't it high time *I* met someone nice?"

Jessica rolled her eyes. "Lila, try not to be so selfish. You go out with dozens of guys!"

"Well," Lila said pouting, "I guess you're right. I guess I really *do* have a pretty outstanding social life."

Jessica groaned as she threw her towel and beach bag into the convertible.

"Hey, Jess, Mr. Collins is waving at you," Lila said, taking her keys out of her bag and strolling over to her lime-green Triumph, parked next to the Fiat. "He looks like he's trying to get your attention."

Jessica frowned. What could Mr. Collins want with her? A minute later she had strolled across the lot to meet him. He was with Teddy, his adorable son, who was covered from head to foot with sand.

"Oh, Jessica," Mr. Collins said, looking at her in confusion. "I'm so sorry. I could have sworn you were Elizabeth. I guess I just saw the Fiat and the blond hair and assumed—"

Jessica felt her face go red. "That's OK," she said. As she walked away, she could hear Teddy saying, "But which one *is* she, Daddy?"

Jessica couldn't believe it. This was the final straw! She had always thought it was a lot of fun being a twin. But not if people couldn't even tell them apart anymore—not if people were just starting to assume she was Elizabeth all the time!

Jessica couldn't stand the thought of losing her

own identity. There was no way she was going to let people think she was Elizabeth. This was getting absurd. She was just going to have to think of some way to make sure no one made that mistake again. Even if it meant doing something unbelievably drastic!

Jessica takes desperate action in Sweet Valley High #32, **THE NEW JESSICA.**

WINNERS

THIS EXCITING NEW SERIES IS ALL ABOUT THE THREE MOST ENVIED, IMITATED AND ADMIRED GIRLS IN MIDVALE HIGH SCHOOL: STACY HARCOURT, GINA DAMONE AND TESS BELDING. THEY ARE WINNERS—GOLDEN GIRLS AND VARSITY CHEERLEADERS—YET NOT EVEN THEY CAN AVOID PROBLEMS WITH BOYFRIENDS, PARENTS, AND LIFE.

☐ **THE GIRL MOST LIKELY (WINNERS #1) 25323/$2.50**

Stacy Harcourt is the captain of the varsity cheerleading squad, but she wants to break from her rigid, boring image as "Miss Perfect." But in doing so will she lose the friendship of Gina and Tess and the captainship of the squad? Or will she realize that maybe her "perfect" life wasn't so bad after all.

☐ **THE ALL AMERICAN GIRL (WINNERS #2) 25427/$2.25**

Gina Damone has problems keeping up socially with the other cheerleaders because of her immigrant parents old-world attitudes. But when she begins dating All-American Dex Grantham his breezy disregard for her parents' rules makes her question his sincerity.

☐ **THE GOOD LUCK GIRL (WINNERS #3)   25644/$2.25**

Cute, cuddly Tess Belding is the first student from Midvale's vocational-technical program ever to make the cheering squad, but she's going to be benched unless she can pass her French midterm!

Prices and availability subject to change without notice.